T0278857

Revolving Door

SEAGULL
BOOKS
•
CELEBRATING
40 YEARS

THE GERMAN LIST

Katja Lange-Müller

Revolving Door

Translated by Simon Pare

LONDON CALCUTTA NEW YORK

This publication has been supported by
a grant from the Goethe-Institut India.

Seagull Books, 2022

Originally published in the German as
Drehtür by Katja Lange-Müller

Copyright © 2017, Verlag Kiepenheuer & Witsch GmbH & Co. KG,
Cologne, Germany

First published in English translation by Seagull Books, 2022
English translation © Simon Pare, 2022

ISBN   978 1 80309 068 9

Typeset by Seagull Books, Calcutta, India
Printed and bound in the USA by Integrated Books International

It seems to me that a human being with the very best of intentions can do immeasurable harm if he is immodest enough to wish to profit those whose spirit and will are concealed from him.

—Friedrich Wilhelm Nietzsche

A flash storm, Asta thinks. I hadn't thought of that word in a long time, but now it's come back to me in a flash. A comely flash? Bullshit. Anyway, a flash storm is a sudden, severe storm that ceases equally abruptly. —'Cease': another word that irritates Asta, interfering with her efforts to recall what might constitute a flash storm. 'Cease' she thinks, could in fact mean something else; but wouldn't you then say 'decease' instead, in my mother tongue, which I haven't forgotten, merely not used in the last 20, no, 22 years I spent where? Away. A way? Oh, way away. —'Mother tongue': this compound noun also kicks off an instant avalanche of associations. The main noun 'mother', previously so distant, now presses up close to her. Main, brain, she thinks; my brain wants me to give it its head and it maintains it has to catch words, in this case German words. Aren't all these German words already encaged inside my headstrong head, 'capital offenders', silent jailbirds who'd long since resigned themselves to their fate; but now I've returned to my native land they're stirring again. —Speaking of mother tongues, how did my mother actually speak and what did she say? No idea, none, not now anyway. The only thing she can remember is why her mother, who died back in 1980, called her Asta. Apparently, her family, no not hers, she's husband- and childless, Mother's family, she wouldn't dream of saying *my* mother, had a pretty, friendly German Shepherd bitch of the same name, and it bore some resemblance to the Danish actress Asta Nielsen. —At least the word 'word' is free, Asta thinks, free of any ambiguity at least, and a flash storm is called

3

a flash storm because it breaks in a flash and ends suddenly, nothing to do with the accompanying flashes of lightning. Is there such a thing as a thunderstorm without lightning? And lightning is followed by thunder, *rolling thunder, thunderclaps*. No thunderstorm without lightning, no lightning without thunder. Otherwise a thunderstorm, even a flash storm, wouldn't be a thunderstorm, just heavy rain. Rein? Reign? In the reign of Queen Dick. Where did I get that expression? From Mother? Maybe—it's certainly stupid enough. 'It never rains but it pours'; 'raining cats and dogs'; strange phrases . . .

And Asta keeps her eyelids shut and rolls her eyeballs back in her skull until they hurt and sees, as if on a cinema screen, crystalline snow-like letters swirling around and clustering and coalescing into legible chains of varying lengths that trickle down almost simultaneously onto her hot, dry tongue and dissolve faster than she could spit out even a single link of these chains. *Chainlink*, thinks Asta, another of those slippery compound words.

I t was a flash storm, a full-on storm with lightning, thunder, rain, and it was already over by the time the old nurse Asta Arnold landed in Munich after a 23-hour journey interrupted by two stopovers, only the last few miles of it buffeted by turbulence; the voice, which has been with her, and sometimes inside her, for about three weeks, knows this. The voice knows what is happening, and even her thoughts are unthinkable without it. The voice decides; it determines what she remembers, sometimes with painful accuracy, sometimes with wistful yearning. The voice guides Asta's eyes, opens her ears and silences her. Let Asta try to resist! For, and the voice is quite powerless against this, what it feeds off, like mistletoe on a tree, is Asta's life—for now, but not for much longer; and when the end comes, it will take them both.

A sta thinks—in silence. Who, she wonders, am I supposed to talk to? I don't know anyone any more, here, on the soil of my fatherland, though it's no longer mine since it no more belongs to me than my mother tongue does; I'm merely standing on it.

Yes, she's standing there, at the eastern end of Level 3 of Franz Josef Strauss airport beside a little-used revolving door, hidden behind a rental car counter, to which her craving for nicotine has blindly led her. A plastic duty-free bag pokes out of Asta's shoulder bag, a stained pigskin monstrosity, and out of the plastic bag pokes a carton of Camels. Her suitcase, they told her at the Iberia airline counter, must have got stuck somewhere during transfer, either in San Salvador or Madrid. This was fairly common, but it would definitely arrive, maybe tomorrow or the day after, next week at the very latest.

In her right hand Asta is holding a newly opened Camel soft pack, the first of ten packets of 20, and a box of Nicaraguan matches, in her left a smouldering cigarette; she draws on it, hard, like someone who hasn't been allowed one for ages, puzzling: Which is accurater: I'm standing in front of the door, or I'm standing behind the door? In front of, behind, accurater . . . One by one, the words, trapped in gas bubbles, seep out of the muddy terrain of the past, gradually filling the pitch-black firmament of my brainpan; and they are floating around up there as sedately as fluffy clouds, semi-transparent but their contours as clear as balloons. I can study each individual word at my leisure, interpret it, possibly understand it. —Accurater? Not all adjectives have a comparative form; this piece of wisdom from her distant school days now pops up on Asta's horizon. What *is* accurate is that she's outside, between the revolving door and a hip-high chrome ashtray brimming with brownish water and soggy cigarette butts. Not a pretty sight, but she doesn't mind. She's having enough trouble getting her bearings; the afternoon summer sun is dazzling her. And what she sees if she doesn't look up into the painfully bright light but to the side, forwards or down, is virtually identical to what she saw as she smoked a couple more farewell cigarettes at Managua airport shortly before take-off: flagstones, concrete pillars, baggage trolleys, the glass front. Here though, thinks Asta, there are a few puddles, from which the sun is guzzling with all its rays, as if through infinitely long straws, as thirstily as a Bedouin camel; the puddles are shrinking before her eyes.

She lights the next cigarette and takes a few steps. Through a high window in the outside wall of the larder and changing room of the Chinese restaurant she passed on her way to the revolving door, she spies a young Asian man in jeans and a somewhat grubby white chef's jacket done up to the chin with black knot buttons, fast asleep in his uncomfortable position across a line of four chairs. His flat, pale face is utterly calm; there's only the occasional twitch of his protruding eyelids and at the corners of his slightly parted lips. He's probably in the middle of a pleasant dream, thinks Asta, and she feels attracted to him precisely because she feels so safe behind the blue-tinted glass, out of reach of the sleeper on the other side. It's not just his dream, she thinks, that sets him apart from me and from this place where both of us find ourselves . . .

Another image slides across the sight of the chef in the larder of the airport's Chinese restaurant. That other man, thinks Asta, was Asian too and, if I guessed correctly, also a chef. When I met him back in the 1970s, I'd just graduated from my nursing course and already signed a contract with that clinic in Leipzig. I was about to leave my tiny flat in the city of my birth, Berlin, which I had never called my hometown, let alone the capital. My move to Leipzig-Plagwitz was dependent only on when my room was vacated at the retirement home for Saxon restaurateurs, which was honestly called Fading Light; the current occupant, a former headwaiter at the Interhotel Astoria, was breathing his final breaths at his daughter Elke's, a nurse I knew from college.

It was on the night of the 20/21 July 1967—an unusually dark night for midsummer. I remember it very clearly because we'd been celebrating Carmen's birthday, as every year. I'd slipped away early, rudely early, with nothing but alcohol in my stomach, as Carmen had once again cooked her casserole *à la thorough turkey*, an inedible sloppy concoction of rice, minced turkey, peas and raisins.

Carmen, the policeman's daughter, the delicate flower, the most beautiful of us all, with whom I'd had almost no contact even before I ran away into the world, and whom I subsequently almost completely forgot; until I found out much later on the internet, one evening after work in Ulan Bator, that a Carmen Meyer, whose birthday coincided more or less fortuitously with my Carmen's, had 'passed away on 15 March 2000 following prolonged and serious illness'. —What might Carmen have died from? Cancer? A stroke? A heart attack? She'd be my age now . . .

8

She had a magnificent shock of red hair, delicate porcelain skin and bottle-green eyes, which—her mother must have been an ignoramus, or the newborn Carmen completely bald—really did not match her fiery first name, giving me, jealous chump that I was, grounds to mock her. Well, one ground at least.

We had argued over a trivial matter that has completely slipped my mind, so I'd stolen away from Carmen's place into the balmy, starless night early enough, albeit fairly drunk and emotional, to do something else and possibly find someone to take to bed. I simply couldn't sober up, though. It was too muggy outside. Insects were swirling around the street lamps' yolk-coloured bulbs, to which I too felt magically attracted, and which would have been risky for me as well, had I been their size and winged. As a girl, and even as a young woman, I'd often longed to be able to fly, to be a moth. —The air was as sticky as the ringlets I'd painstakingly curled into my hair at home and later—in Carmen's kitchen; she didn't have a bathroom, none of us did—misted with so much Western hairspray that they stood out from my skull as stiffly as sculpted concrete; I could have shaken my head for minutes and not a single hair would have broken free of the others. —A thunderstorm was in the air, but it didn't break over this part of Berlin, the northeast, but moved on—no idea where to.

I walked the whole way home and had just reached the desolate administrative area we called 'Dead End' because it was totally bleak in the evenings and at the weekends seemed eerily quiet—as I said, *dead*—and was crossing Otto Nuschke Strasse near where it forks left into Glinkastrasse when I saw him. Or did I only hear him at first? An animal whimpering pitifully, I assumed, a dog maybe . . .

The human, a man of Asian origin as I then discerned through the gloom, was crouching in a doorway. I stopped and murmured a few inconsequential words I no longer recall, and yet they, or more likely my husky voice, wrested from his throat a sound that was simultaneously high-pitched and deep.

I can hear the sob or whatever it was now; it must have lodged in my ear at the time and has been waiting ever since for my memory to find and press the right button.

Aloud—there's no such thing as 'aquiet', only quietly aloud—it sounded or sounds as if the man couldn't hold it back a second longer, however hard he clenched his lips. So godforsaken, so cosmically forlorn.

'Do you need help?' I asked; but he carried on weeping. I crouched down beside him and touched his shoulder, and he automatically turned his face to mine. His already fleshy eyelids were so swollen that he could barely lift them; but when he did manage to do so, his pupils glittered surreally through the slanted, fractionally open slits. As I whispered at him, my mouth inches from his nose, he probably smelt my wine-soured breath, then lowered his hands, which were hovering near his mouth like the half-veil of an oriental woman, and laid his right index finger against his badly swollen left cheek. His skin, which looked ash-grey even in the warm yellow lamplight, was stretched taut from the lower edge of his eyelid to his chin over a large bump. Of course, I realized, he has toothache!

It never ceases to amaze, does it, that a grown adult, every last inch of him, can be boiled down to a tiny red thread, the rebellious nerve of his tooth?!

He tried to dodge me, banging his head on the door behind him and lurching to one side, but he couldn't escape. I pressed my left hand to his forehead, which was boiling even though the rest of him was as pale as a corpse, and I grabbed his arm, I've no idea why. Sure,

I was still drunk, obviously frustrated, and apart from his swollen cheek he looked exotic enough, very good-looking in fact—slim, young, needy. But he was headstrong too, warding me off and refusing to allow me to pull him to his feet. So I got even closer and more intimate, cupping his face in my hands and forcing him to look at me. Maybe the decisive and empathetic nature of my actions stirred something inside him, a desire for consolation. For his mum? His tears started to flow more freely again, but the noises accompanying the tears were more muffled now, more heartfelt, though no less plaintive. I rubbed his eyes with the hem of my ankle-length flowery cotton dress; any more and I'd have wiped away a shiny string of snot dangling from his nose, which is completely normal when someone's crying so hard.

I kept up my insistent patter, and although he didn't understand a single word, he seemed to realize I meant him no harm. Or was it simply my touch that broke his resistance or perhaps even soothed him?

As I wanted to have at least some kind of conversation with him, I imitated toothache, furrowing my brow, patting my cheek, parting my lips, tapping my tongue, closing my mouth again, swallowing and moaning as if the pill were beginning to take effect. And he did in fact get to his feet and let me lead him—no, march him!—away like a wrongdoer who had recognized the inescapability of his situation and surrendered. I pulled him by the hand, which was slender and firm and cold, along the street, into the hallway and up the stairs. We'd just reached the door of my flat and I was rummaging in my bag for the keys when he made one last escape bid, running back down to the third floor, but he turned back when he heard my key in the lock.

We went into my single room, and he sat down on my upholstered chair, a huge, comfy wing chair I'd bought for ten 'tin chips', as we called East German marks, from a permanently penniless local alkie. I got a bottle of strong brandy from the fridge, dug out a pack of Titretta painkillers and tossed it between the two schnapps glasses that were standing on the table in front of him as if they'd been expecting us. He unscrewed the bottle, poured a little—only for himself, mind you—, drank, nodded, refilled his glass and drank again, holding the bottle in his other hand as he did so until I gently removed it from his grip, served us both and chinked my glass against his before drinking from mine.

'Prost,' I said, and taking back the bottle, he uttered his only word that night: 'Gombee'.

He answered my blank look with a quick, lopsided smile. As far as I can recall, he didn't smile again.

Now, our encounter was what some might call brief; right now, though, it strikes me as having been so long and so intense because I'm having a kind of déjà-vu that expands every detail to surreal proportions.

We sat there drinking, he more than I. Again I attempted to talk to him, but he didn't understand Russian, the only language other than German with which I was familiar back then, or even the three or four English phrases everyone knows. What else could I do? I went back to basics, pounded my chest and said, 'Asta', then made circles with my finger in front of his chest, pulled a quizzical face and my shoulders up, and spread my arms.

He understood what I wanted from him; of that I was and am convinced.

His eyes widened, he stared fearfully into space, shook his head and waved dismissively. It was fairly clear that he no more wished to reveal his name than the place he'd fled from with his raging toothache.

I demonstrated my job by pretending to wrap a bandage around my foot, take my own blood and insert a syringe. At the end of my performance I drew a cross in the air. Even as I made this cross, though, I started to have my doubts. Maybe, I thought, he doesn't take me for the nurse I am, but for a pious Christian acting like a Samaritan in order to convert him.

Even though he didn't smile this time, my second short silent film appeared to amuse him. Or rouse him? Now he too mimed a variety of activities, chopping up non-existent vegetables, stirring an imaginary pan with which he tossed an equally imaginary object into the air and caught it again.

Excitedly, I rushed into the kitchen and returned with a pot, a plate and unfortunately a big, sharp knife as well. There was a fresh flicker of terror in his eyes—I've no idea whether he was scared of me and the knife or by the fact that he had carelessly divulged his job.

That was the end—of everything except for the drinking. I lost all desire. I was still thinking of my bed, sure, but no longer of how to lure him into it. I was bored by his fear, his toothache, which the alcohol was obviously doing a wonderful job of dulling, his sheer stubborn sadness and his obstinate wariness of strangers; tiredness crept into my bones and weighed down my eyelids.

Had I really been intending to have sex with this fleeting acquaintance? Am I claiming so after the event because I'm keen to talk myself up, or down, as what used to be referred to as a 'bit of all right'? Could it be that now, almost 50 years later, I'm embarrassed that I succumbed to com*passion*, however strange that now sounds, and merely wished to help and, only if an opportunity were to arise, to scrounge a few crumbs of happiness for myself, a quickie, a few kisses or at least a grateful, admiring glance?! Might my memory of the young Asta, of myself that is, be a legend fuelled by self-loathing and narcissism?

I left him sitting there with my schnapps, or rather *his* by now, slumped on the bed as I was, in my flowery dress, curled up and fell asleep.

When the clatter of dustbins being emptied woke me the next morning, the light was still on. But he was gone—and so was the bottle of brandy. I padded into the kitchen and then into the hallway, where I found the front door shut, then back into the room to see if anything other than him and the bottle had disappeared. But since for now nothing was missing, I took off my clothes and took myself off to bed again.

Hours later—it might have been around 12 o'clock—I heard an insistent knock on the door. Luckily I was already showered and in my dressing gown and had just made myself some coffee; that was the only reason I went to open up. Or did I perhaps think that my patient, having taken only a nearly empty bottle of brandy with him, might have forgotten something after all?

Outside my door, however, was neither the man himself nor one Asian. No, there were six like him out there. They were wearing grey-green uniforms, and one of them presented me with a bunch of white roses.

'Frau Arnold,' the one on the far left, the one with the bouquet, said in perfect German, 'thank you! You took exemplary care of our sick comrade, and your fine socialist sister country is an ally of ours. However, being out in the streets of your glorious capital city and so close to the Anti-Fascist Protective Rampart alone at night is not without its dangers. Allow us therefore to present these modest flowers in the name of our great leader Kim Il-Sung and the entire Democratic People's Republic of Korea.'

He read out these lines, which I think I remember verbatim, particularly the 'modest flowers' bit, from a piece of paper. I didn't say anything in response, except maybe 'Bye', grabbed the bouquet and, after the gentlemen had done some quick bowing, swiftly closed the door of my flat, which I then bolted, I think, once they had reached the bottom of the building or at least once their steps had stopped echoing in the staircase.

I sat down in the same upholstered chair in which my night-time guest had sat, reached for the pack of Clubs lying next to the empty Titretta box and, with trembling hands, lit a match. Its flame blackened the cigarette, which I forgot to draw on until it almost scorched my fingertips.

A Korean—so that's what he was; and a North Korean to boot! I might have figured that out, especially as that peculiar country's consulate was in Glinkastrasse, not far from my house, if, yes, *if* I'd been capable of figuring anything out. Who or what else could he have been?! Chinese, Japanese, Mongolian, Vietnamese, Thai? Why had I guessed all sorts of other nationalities but not Korean? His complexion was dark and yet pale, his face less rounded than Mongolian, Chinese and Japanese faces, his nose large and proudly arched, his hair bristly and thick but dark brown rather than blue-black. Bleached by kitchen steam maybe? Overall he looked more like an indió, South, Central or North American; I could easily have taken him for Mexican, Bolivian or even Sioux.

And how, I wondered, had his countrymen turned up on my doormat so fast. They knew my name, my address ... Had they been watching us or merely tailing him, this party comrade and embassy chef, who had somehow been driven crazy by severe toothache, and who had probably tried to nurse himself with schnapps before we even met—in his workplace between the baskets of vegetables and woks, or in his attic room under the consulate roof, and under a poster of the dictator, surrounded by happy workers, men in grey-green fabric and women in garish robes and laughing young pioneers? Or had he, knowing that his presumably unauthorized absence had been noted, denounced himself and announced, without delay, where he'd been, why, for how long and with whom? Will they simply mete out some harsh discipline, or is he already on his way back to his far-off, ferocious homeland where 20 to 30 years in a gulag await? Or a life sentence? Or worse?

What about me? Are they going to tip off the Ministry for State Security? Will I be able to talk my way out of it if our lot calls me in? I'll spin them some drivel about solidarity and that, as a nurse, I see it as my duty to help any person at any time.

Nothing happened, though, absolutely nothing. I received no visit from our own officials—or any un-officials—and for my diplomatic neighbours the case was closed as far as I was concerned.

Realizing that I'd played a not inconsiderable role in the young embassy chef's future fate, I crept around the North Korean residence, a forbidding concrete block completed only a few years previously, two or three more times under cover of darkness, but I saw no one but the guard standing by his sentry box.

I told myself that some stories in a person's life—also, or perhaps especially, in my own—were destined to remain unresolved, and if I couldn't put up with the suspense, I'd have to dream up my own plot and conclusion.

All of a sudden Asta hears sounds, real sounds; shrill but not entirely tuneless singing brings her back to reality. She spins round towards what she presumes to be the source of the singing and catches sight of a man in threadbare yellowish elephant-cord trousers bending over a rubbish bin, shovelling paper, bottles, plastic bags, crushed drink cans and half-eaten food out of it with both hands, and dumping it all on the ground.

Lounge bottoms, she recalls; that was our name for that style of trousers, and the next moment she remembers the joke that brought it to mind. Paul comes home late and a little drunk. Paula, he says to his wife, I went to the doctor's today. He wants to re-examine me tomorrow morning. I'm supposed to take along a urine sample, a stool sample and a sperm sample, all at once. Where's the problem? Paula replies. Just put on your favourite cords again.

A loose T-shirt dangles down to the man's knees, its colour best described as washed-out blue. But 'washed-out' would be misleading because the dirty, crumpled piece of clothing has dark patches edged with white salt lines, under the armpits; an odour of sweat, both fresh and old, stings Asta's nose, even though the man keeps his distance. His black hair, already slightly greying but only at the front, is long, thick and crazy—like his eyes. The full, chapped lips in the middle of his sunburnt, angular face form only sounds, not words, or at least none that Asta is capable of deciphering. She thinks she can make out the tune of 'Lightly row'.

When did I last hear that? she wonders. If he wasn't humming that nursery rhyme, I'd think he was a Nicaraguan, a Nica, as they call themselves and we called them too, one of those who rooted around in the rubbish heaps of Managua, Léon or Rivas and then ended up there themselves after starving or being beaten to death. Some, though, the ones who were less apathetic or more fortunate, ended up with us; one brought in his feverish child, one had meningitis, one arthritis, one an ear infection, another worms and yet another had trodden on a scorpion; many of them we could help, but not every one.

Helping—was that what it was? It was! But did the misery begin with the helping? Or the other way around: the helping with the misery? Helping, helping, helping, and why? Is it something we always need, I needed? Or was I trying to prove something else without quite knowing what it was? And to whom was I trying to prove this 'something else'? To myself? To our patients? Sure, most of us were and are doctors, nurses and carers from Western Europe, the United States, Canada, Japan . . . more useful—Doctor Nieswandt would say 'more effective'—than our often poorly trained colleagues in developing countries and the world's crisis or disaster zones. Did we hope, do we hope, perhaps unconsciously, that the people who benefited from our skills, possibilities and drugs, and who will continue to benefit from them—*benefit*, another completely stupid word—therefore believe we're superior to them, not just in medicine but in virtually every domain? Don't our actions, even though many of us think of ourselves as atheists, have a missionary-like dimension? On the other hand, the desire, indeed the sense of duty, to help a fellow is an age-old reflex—and the sole preserve of our own species.

I was 19 and had just moved into my place in Leipzig when I came home one mid-September day after the early shift to find my room strangely dark. The space between the panes of my closed double windows was, I quickly realized, teeming with so many wasps that they almost blocked out the light. Since I had no reason to fear their stings, I inspected the little animals very calmly and compared them with the species depicted in my insect guide. The species before me was the German wasp, which, the guide said, 'is a sociable creature whose wings are folded at rest. It nests in dark nooks and is capable in one life cycle of producing a population of up to 50,000 individuals.'

My German wasps had built their nest in an empty space between the outside wall and the window frame and, in attempting to build out from there, must have chewed their way through mortar and wood—and encountered nothing but air. Or a transparent jail, rather, for even *Vespula germanica* is incapable of gnawing through glass.

I waited until dusk, as all swarming insects including wasps return to their homes then, and once mine had gone to sleep or were at least out of sight, I squeezed a whole bottle of washing-up liquid into the opening they'd made for crawling in and out; I thought this would kill them.

But what disaster met my eyes the next morning, a Sunday! Different-sized groups of detergent-smeared wasps were dragging sodden or poisoned comrades out of the hole and manoeuvring them onto the windowsill, where other clusters and gangs of walking wounded were frantically doing their best to help their badly contaminated friends, cleaning them with their mandibles and prising apart their sticky wings. It was horrific, and not only because I now truly understood just how 'sociable' these yellow-and-black-striped nuisances really were.

On Monday morning I related my misadventures to Margit the night nurse and as she took off her uniform and put on her trench coat, she dictated over the ward telephone the number of a pest-control expert, whom, much to my surprise, I immediately got through to. And since I had promised him a healthy sum if he could come quickly, he found time for me that same evening and put an end to the suffering.

Oh yes, helping was nice, thinks Asta—to begin with. What about later? Later, years later, one of my trainee nurses said it 'turns you on'. The phrase didn't sit well with me, even if it is pretty accurate: helping turns you on. It's a turn-on. A powerful turn-on. Helping stirs a strange desire inside you, and yet the way it can be satisfied in such intoxicating fashion makes you want to do it over and over again. It might even bring comfort, and not just to the needy, but above all it's a challenge, very much in the sporting sense of the word. If you're called—or for that matter, empowered—to help, it's comforting and challenging to encounter someone in a worse state than yourself; better still: a far worse state. You're instantly flooded with a warm emotional soup whose principal ingredients are pity and an urge to act—and derision, a superiority-fuelling derision, for which many, both professional and amateur helpers, also secretly deride themselves. As a professional working for Médecins sans Frontières or CARE International for example, patients come to you on whom other people, their family or the village elder or a miracle worker, have long since given up, the patients they could no longer help—or didn't want to. And if these hopeless cases survived our professional help, at least temporarily, they might remain, though undoubtedly less sick, at best just about healthy enough to survive. For there's no such thing as full health, complaint-free health, least of all in the health service.

You can't serve health. You can serve tea, you can serve people, but health? I'm not sure what to imagine.

Nevertheless, the sick and even, if need be, those who are just about clinging on, give you—nurse, carer or doctor—the greatest and grandest feeling, maybe the biggest turn-on of all: the power to help, helper power in fact, and an even more powerful, sometimes even overpowering power to experience respect and admiration—boundless admiration—from all sides.

But all this helping is risky, titillatingly so. You're always teetering on the brink of failure, for your efforts frequently prove futile, but forgiveness is not always forthcoming, not even from yourself. In return, on the other side of that fine line, as a kind of compensation, is earthly sainthood. If you're lucky—or unlucky—those you help, whose pain you were actually able to relieve, and especially those emergency patients who no longer feel anything, no pain anyway or at least not the original physical pain, will venerate you or even love you. —And don't worry, they'll find other needy people dying to put you and your abilities to the test. It costs you energy and generally doesn't pay, not financially anyway. And because they didn't die, they won't let you die either, least of all the poor and the poorest. Gratitude is not eternal but it's surprisingly resilient, and hope is as strong as an ox and famously the last thing to die.

'Hope is the last thing to die, but it does.' Ward sister Elisabeth, who always had a whiff of herbal liqueur about her, uttered these disarmingly sober words in the closed women's psychiatric unit of Berlin-Herzberge clinic, my favourite training ward, after she caught the three trainee nurses, Susanne, Monika and me, attempting to make a catatonically depressed patient laugh.

Idiotic boffins call the need to assist other members of the same species—a need we share with many creatures, even such lowly and disagreeable animals as wasps and ants—'helper syndrome', as if it were a multi-faceted and complex disease, a psycho-epidemic affecting only members of our own species. What on earth is sick about wanting to see our fellow men healthy—or dead, if it's impossible to heal them? Where would the world be if every medical professional were suddenly cured of this so-called helper syndrome or if they lost it for good?! The greatest disaster ever witnessed would sweep the cities and villages, forests and steppes and deserts of every country on our degenerate planet.

If worse comes to worst, I'd prefer to be dead—which will happen sooner or later anyway—than sick; I mean properly, seriously sick, wasting away in agony, suffering unto the grave. Death is preferable to sickness—for the sick person, at least; less so, naturally, for those who go on living, the people who stood, or rather sat, by the *departed*, around their deathbed, in a clinic or an old people's home or in their own home—on the edge of the plastic sheet protecting one—or to be more precise his—half of the conjugal bed from all the excretions and other bodily fluids of which he'd lost control shortly before being permitted to exit the stage. These bereaved relatives fret almost as much as the terminally ill person before he escaped from his serious illness—a state of being no longer here but not yet gone. Who has the generosity of spirit to simply rejoice, from the bottom of their hearts if they so wish, for the 'beloved relative, sorely missed' as graveside speakers would have it, whose hard-won death the obituaries will later describe as a 'release'. It's possible that occasionally someone is genuinely beloved, even in the final stages and beyond death; but love alone—on this we pros are unanimous— is of little use to someone who, as Nurse Elisabeth puts it, 'has boarded Charon's boat'. That person deserves care, preferably loving care, but what they really need is unemotional, skilled, professional nursing care.

B rooding and oblivious to her surroundings, Asta has made her way along the glass front, but now she has her eye on the large store at the left-hand corner of Terminal I. Super, she thinks, a supermarket. Why shouldn't such things now exist in Germany too, at this airport even? She peers through the window, takes a long drag on her cigarette and wonders if she has other cravings than for nicotine, perhaps for something to eat, something typically German. What might she fancy? What speciality has she missed or at least not eaten for a long time? *Gutsleberwurst*, Asta thinks, and the thought tickles her. What, in flaming Judas Priest, is a good sliver sausage? She knows, though, that a Gutsleberwurst is simply a liver sausage, but again she's at sixes and sevens with her mother tongue despite her mastery of it. Or its of her? And yet still she wrestles with all these words, not one of which has actually passed her lips since she returned to the land of the Germans and German. But even unspoken and indeed unheard, again and again or still, her German words sound oddly alien to her ears, especially the compound or, more like, compressed nouns of this language that can be wound into garlands many metres long: *Gutsleberwurstkonsumentenbefragungsbögenauswertungsanalyseschlüssel-bereitstellungsersuchen . . .*

Oh yes, Asta has quite a precise memory of the consistency, smell and taste of Gutsleberwurst, which used to be her favourite sausage back home. Soft, she says to herself, Gutsleberwurst is soft; you can slather it on to a sliver of bread because it's mainly forcemeat, what the French call *farce*. But a farce is also a coarse play, a spectacle. Probably because the characters in such plays were 'scoffed at', 'taken to the cleaners' or even 'put through the grinder'. Only symbolically, mind you. The Germans call a grinder a *Wolf*. Why? Does the minced meat and liver—or sliver?—look like the contents of a wolf's stomach? Like Little Red Riding Hood and her grandmother? But they climbed out of the wolf's stomach in best fairy-tale fashion, intact and unscathed. —A spectacle? That's right, it also contains speck, as in lard: strips and chunks of speck, not in the spectacle or the fairy tale but in the sausage; pieces of speck and liver, big and small; pieces of calf, cow, pig or chicken liver; and these pieces please not theatregoers but the tongue. The sausage meat is pressed into intestines and cured; Gutsleberwurst smells good and tastes good, of smoke, marjoram, thyme and mace, and a little of liver too.

If I were hungry and had some euros, I might go into that airport supermarket and buy something, a Gutsleberwurst or something else, taste it and thus, with my tongue of course, 'get a toehold' in this place again, however acrobatic that might sound. But I'm not hungry. You lose all sense of hunger working yourself into the ground nursing a bunch of half-starved people. An appetite at least? You lose that too from eating the hospital food we all shared and which was uniformly bland, even when for once it didn't consist of donated coconut fat, maize flour and corned beef.

Actually, going out to eat was some of my colleagues' favourite pastime. Whenever they had a couple of hours off, they would change into casual clothes and scour the areas around our walk-in clinics for a restaurant or at least a 'great snack bar', as they called the less gastronomic locations. However ruined, bleak or dangerous the neighbourhood, Anton, Beate, Clarisse, Dr Duraty and Dr Nieswandt sincerely regarded these 'dens of gluttony', most of them astronomically expensive with a sideline in bootleg alcohol or moonshine, as 'well-kept secrets', although they were mainstream rather than an insider tip. It wasn't just our lot who hung out in such places. Parasites from all branches of the crisis industry were regulars too: mercenaries, spies, reporters, pharmaceutical sales reps, dealers, scavengers, prostitutes and shady profiteers who could arrange, in exchange for cash, anything a foreigner's heart desired: brandy, cigars, guns, antiques, junk cars, rip-off branded clothing, lipstick . . .

Why do I need euros? I'm sure I could pay by card. Sure? It's not that sure, especially for small sums. Get out my credit card 'for peanuts' and the till attendant would give me an earful. I'd need a comeback, something to 'set things straight', even if she isn't really out of line, the woman over there who occasionally glances up as she scans the items the conveyor belt ferries towards her, blowing her long blue-and-green-streaked fringe out of her eyes and staring into the air with ostentatious seriousness—that, and maybe her white uniform, make her look like Tamara. Tamara, who always wore such bright clothes under the obligatory nurse's scrubs, the cocky hippie child of a Hamburg shipping magnate's daughter, who in Tamara's words 'never really grew up, not even as an old biddy', and the 'prematurely red-faced son of an eastern Westphalian shop owner'. As Tamara very plausibly deduced, she owed, or rather begrudged, her name to her dad's infatuation with the Cuban Revolution and, in particular, with Che Guevara's sister-in-arms Tamara Bunke.

Tamara Schröder, a specialist neurological and psychiatric nurse, whose tireless zeal may indeed have been driven by helper syndrome . . . With the exception of our colleagues, who couldn't stand *me* either, everyone liked her, especially our young patients, not just because, depending on her mood, her hair might be blue, green, purple or dark-orange but also because she had Castro, a real-life polychromatic parrot who spoke not a word, nor of English or German, and was as colourful a character as she was. Tamara made no effort to educate him, but he did come to work with her until the threat of avian flu hovered over us.

Was Tamara some kind of involuntary clown or more of a female Buster Keaton? Tamara with her garish mop and poker face, who despite repeatedly denying that she identified a little, well quite a lot actually, with the German-born Argentinian Haydée Tamara Bunke Bíder, a.k.a. Tania la Guerillera, knew everything there was to know about her. And when Tamara spoke, or rather lectured us, about her namesake for the umpteenth time for hours on end, it was never entirely clear whether she was telling Tamara Bunke's story or one she had somehow appropriated.

Her father was a sports teacher; her mother, a Ukrainian Jew, also taught, and they were both ardent Communists who were forced to emigrate from Germany in 1935 and returned from their Argentinian exile only in 1952. Due to their convictions, however, they did not go to West Germany but took Olaf, their firstborn, of whom the only thing we know is that he became a mathematician, and their daughter Tamara, who had first clapped eyes on the world—or rather the world on her—in Buenos Aires on 19 November 1937, to the German Democratic Republic, initially to Stalinstadt, a kind of architectural laboratory for real industrial workers that was later renamed Eisenhüttenstadt when Uncle Joe's crimes led to his being toppled from his pedestal.

Although their home was a horrible unfinished flat the Bunke family had to share with three fellow teachers, and Tamara had as yet gained no real view of the world, in the fullness of time she adopted her parents' Marxist-Leninist worldview and this was consolidated by spells at boarding school and in the GST, the Sport and Technology Association, a paramilitary organization with uniforms and stuff. Tamara practised shooting every day in the GST compound and soon won competitions and cups that served to prop up books by Marx, Engels and Lenin in the Hellerau-made wall unit.

However, the wretched living conditions in Stalinstadt got Dad and Mum Bunke down and so they applied to the Grey Monastery, a former Prussian high school. They were greeted with open arms and moved to central Berlin, which is where they had first met in 1933, the year of the Nazi takeover, prior to those 17 years in exile.

Tamara, an ambitious girl, pursued her beloved shooting in the East German capital, learnt to play the accordion, the piano and the guitar and passed her high-school diploma in 1956, not at the Grey Monastery, however—she would have considered that 'too bourgeois'—but at Clara Zetkin High School.

In 1958 Tamara began to study Romance languages at Berlin's Humboldt University. Probably out of homesickness, she founded the Ernst Thälmann German-Latin American Youth Group, fell in love with tango and traditional folk music, applied, bizarrely and simultaneously, both to join the Socialist Unity Party of Germany and, apparently tormented by either genuine or imaginary nostalgia, to be released from her East German citizenship and permitted to leave for Argentina.

Tamara was accepted into the Party but not released for the time being, not from her East German nationality nor to go to Argentina. No one, however, could deprive her of her good contacts to her former homeland and to other Latin Americans studying in the GDR. Tamara was also electrified by the reports that had been trickling in from Cuba since 1957, and her desire to see a real revolution quickly developed into an obsession. She wanted the same thing—armed insurrection—for Argentina or at least to be allowed to fight in Cuba.

Lo and behold, in 1960, the year she was given the number 430/60 as a mole for the Main Directorate for Reconnaissance, the foreign intelligence service of the East German Ministry of State Security, chance lent her a helping hand—if indeed it *was* chance. Ernesto Guevara, still the director of the Cuban National Bank, visited the socialist half of Germany, and who but Comrade Bunke should be appointed to be his interpreter. No more than that, though, insisted Tamara Schröder, who cannot possibly have been a witness: Bunke and Che Guevara were never lovers, as malicious gossip would later have it; her charismatic countryman did, however, make a lasting impression on the beautiful Tamara and nourished the revolutionary bee in her bonnet.

Since she was not allowed to go to Argentina but still wanted to do some proper fighting rather than simply indulging in agitprop, Tamara seized the first opportunity to come her way. While interpreting for the Cuban National Ballet in early May 1961, she travelled on the dance company's train to Prague via Dresden.

DeDeRonis, as the Czechs referred to the inmates of the next-door Deutsche Demokratische Republik, could get that far without any trouble.

Tamara and the Cuban prima ballerina became friends, and Tamara eventually screwed up her courage and confided in her. Somehow or other, the two young women managed to trick—or seduce—the director of the Prague State Opera. Slender, well-toned Tamara, she of the smouldering gaze, spoke such perfect Spanish that he saw little risk in issuing her a plane ticket under a pseudonym Tamara had invented. A pernicious myth, however, claims that Tamara took the seat of a dancer who'd run away during this trip to Europe, the company's first, and an even nastier legend has it that to fulfil her most fervent wish, she slept with a secretary from the Cuban embassy in Prague.

Be that as it may: on 12 May 1961 Tamara and the *señorita ballerinas* landed in Havana. It is unclear to this day whether the Ministry of State Security, whose 'unofficial collaborator' she still was—it's only a small step from Argentine to agent, although she would undoubtedly have rather made that step in the opposite direction—knew all along and turned a blind eye, or was fooled. According to the West German Federal Intelligence Service's minutes of their interrogation of Tamara's handler, the Stasi Oberleutnant Günter Männel, who had defected in 1961 on account of two offences, drunk driving and sexual assault, Tamara's operations in the 'non-socialist economic area' had been scheduled to take place later, with Argentina or the US mentioned as possible destinations. But so soon before his own act of betrayal, Männel might already have been *burnt*, as it is known in intelligence jargon, and the latest changes to the 'Career Plans for UC 430/60' may therefore have been withheld from him. What is clear is that Tamara had managed to escape the Stasi's control. Or might they have been pulling the strings all along?

Tamara studied journalism at Havana University and continued her interpreting, although now she worked exclusively for the victorious revolutionary government. Naturally—once a spy, always a spy—Tamara was trained in military and conspiratorial techniques by the DGI, the Cuban Ministry for State Security. She joined the government-sponsored National Revolutionary Militia in 1962, chose Tania as her nom de guerre and always appeared in uniform thereafter. Her DGI handler Ulises Estrada, who wrote a book titled *Tania: With Che in the Bolivian Underground* after her death, won Tamara's heart. 'It was,' Estrada wrote, 'a deep and secret love that endured for decades, undimmed by time and space.' But according to his account, there was no evidence that Tamara, alias Tania, had ever shown anything more than fraternal feelings towards any other comrade.

As soon as she had completed her training as a Cuban agent, Tamara travelled on fake passports across Europe, even entering West Berlin once. Sensing her impending fate, did she seize the chance to pay one last visit to her parents in the Friedrichshain area of East Berlin? They have never confirmed it, at any rate.

In 1964, immediately after her European tour, the DGI dispatched Tamara to Bolivia under the pseudonym Laura Gutiérrez Bauer. She was to make contact with the upper classes and gain their trust, a task she carried out to perfection; she was after all extremely intelligent and charming, as well as being stunningly good looking, of course. Yet as Tamara—or Tania as we now know her—made use of all her contacts to fulfil her grand dream of armed struggle, she learnt that her idol Che Guevara was also in Bolivia and had begun preparations for a guerrilla war. She therefore decided not to inform the DGI, who were only ever interested in exploiting her feminine charms, and finally to heed her desire to emulate Joan of Arc by striking out alone for Che's secret base whose approximate coordinates she must have elicited from Ulises.

Before vanishing for ever Tamara abandoned her four-by-four on the edge of the jungle along with a thick notebook bursting with intel. As she had evidently planned, the Bolivian military discovered them both. On 21 March 1967, the day the soldiers found Tamara's jeep, her identity was uncovered, just as she had intended, and suddenly the DGI was one agent light. Or was it? In any case, Tamara successfully slogged her way, all on her own, to Che and his troops.

However, as she had fallen ill during her strenuous rainforest trip, contracting a serious fever, she was not allowed to move on immediately with the comandante, who disapproved of her 'undisciplined actions', and was forced, at Che's behest and against her will, to stay behind with Juan Vitalio Acuña Nuñes, known as Vilo.

This rearguard under Vilo's command was plagued by rotten luck. Their radio sets packed in in the humid heat, and they lost touch with Che and his comrades. Vilo, Tamara and their comrades-in-arms advanced into a battle for which they were even worse prepared than for revolution—an out-and-out battle for survival. For Tamara, having so craved this moment, it was her very first battle, but for all of them it was to be their worst and their last. The guerrilleros lost their bearings and wandered the eastern slopes of the Andes in scattered groups for months. They had no provisions left and barely any ammunition, not enough to hunt wild animals. The rainforest critters bit and stung them, and they never managed to rejoin the main group or even repair their radio sets.

On 31 August 1967, along with those remaining comrades who had not already perished of starvation or fallen victim to malaria, Tamara Bunke and Vilo died in an enemy ambush on the Río Grande near Puerto Mauricio. Seven days later, fishermen recovered 12 bodies that had been disfigured beyond all recognition.

Ulises writes that Tamara's rucksack contained a 'tightly folded' half-written letter, which was somehow later delivered to her parents or we would have no knowledge of Tamara's final words:

'Dear Mother, I'm scared. I don't know what will become of me and the others. Probably nothing. I don't know what will become of me. Probably nothing. I try to remember what it's like to be brave. I am nothing. I'm no longer even a woman or a girl, just a child . . .'

T hat, thinks Asta, was more or less how Tamara had repeatedly told that story, usually to me and with particular relish when we were on the night shift together. Once, though—for once, all was quiet on our child oncology ward in Timișoara, Easter was approaching, and we were sharing a two-litre bottle of red wine that a farmer had sold me directly from the back of his lorry—Tamara Schröder's story didn't end where Tamara Bunke's had. That early morning—the bottle was by then half-empty—she let another cat out of the bag. Her own.

'For a few years,' Tamara began, 'I wasn't a nurse—not any more and not yet again. You see, I used to be a writer and indeed published a novel that received some decent reviews from several German news-papers. It's about a woman whose role model is Tamara Bunke and who is also called, or calls herself, Tamara; I deliberately left that open. This Tamara, a kind of groupie of the historical Tamara, is as devoted to the revolution as her idol was and as I was at the time. She tries to shake the people around her out of their complacency and get them off their spoilt arses. Not due to some inner urge, though; no, she simply wants to live up to the image she has created of Tamara Bunke.'

I've never seen this book. Now, though, I would have the chance and, more importantly, the time to chase up Tamara Schröder's novel in an antiquarian bookshop or somewhere, if it genuinely exists and isn't just another of her tall tales, and maybe I'll even read it. Am I really going to take up things now that I never found interesting before, simply because I suddenly have time on my hands? How much time do I actually have left?

'After that first novel,' Tamara continued, 'I tried my best to write a second and at some stage I realized I wouldn't be able to pull it off again, having already exhausted the only material capable of wringing words from me. It was then, as the only possible way out of this dead-end, this failure or whatever it might have been, that I decided I would no longer seek to rouse humankind with words but to serve it instead, effectively shaming it through my goodness, and would therefore return to the profession I had trained for. Perhaps I was hoping to become a sort of anti-Tamara, a Tamara by other means, one who pursues her ideals peacefully, preferably in Latin America of course, like Tamara Bunke, or in some other remote crisis-hit region with which I feel a greater affinity than I do towards the sleepy country of my birth. I owe being able to glimpse and pursue this path—or escape route, if you prefer—to an Indian lady.'

For her novel—unless I'm mistaken it's called *Who's Basking in Tamara Bunke's Shadow?*—Tamara Schröder was summoned to the Frankfurt Book Fair 'to do a couple of press events', as she put it. 'And on the final day,' she said, 'within the final few minutes in fact—I was trying to say goodbye to the publishing staff who had to pack up all the printed material—when I had an encounter that would mark another turning point in my life.' Tamara drained her glass, I refilled it and then she really got going.

'When this tall man with grey curly hair—I think he was the programme director of the book fair—walked into the hall, he looked pretty friendly at first sight, not at all like your typical cultural manager, more like a prematurely ageing, slightly overweight amateur rocker who doesn't much enjoy his day job as an executive running the fair but is nevertheless sufficiently professional and ambitious to squeeze into an Armani suit from time to time.

' "Oh, how glad I am, Frau Schröder, that at least you're still here!" the man cried, waddling towards me with his arms spread wide like an albatross's wings. "The authors from India, which is this year's guest of honour, have just complained bitterly to me because, as you may be aware, I worked for the German Foreign Ministry in New Delhi until last year. Our Indian friends felt neglected and said that they'd had no contact with other colleagues, let alone any German writers, and had received very little recognition of their needs. Only once, they said, have they been taken on an open-top bus tour of Frankfurt and invited to dinner by the German Booksellers' Association. And so, my dear, my esteemed Frau Schröder, you extraordinarily talented and politically engaged young author, I'm now trying my best to arrange a get-together, a small, informal meeting with some of our Indian guests. Seven of them are still here. Each of you will read two or three pages of his or her work in English, and if anyone would rather not do so him- or herself, then I will gladly step in. And then we'll have a chat. I will chair it. I don't believe that anything of yours has been published in English yet, has it? Never mind, that is the least of our problems. We'll have something translated quickly. If necessary I'll do it myself, even if it means staying up half the night. Please say yes, a spontaneous yes. That would be absolutely fantastic. The whole thing won't last very long, either. We'll book you a nice hotel room. Many are free again now. And you'll also be paid a small fee . . . "

'He kept badgering me in similar fashion and at similar speed, oblivious to the fact that I was already inclined to say yes. I had some sympathy with the Indians for feeling put out. People hadn't really been scrambling to see me either, and I knew as little about Indian literature as I did in general about a country where so many beautiful, unhappy women live. I'd seen photos of some of those Indian women with sad eyes wearing splendid saris while I was leafing through an illustrated book that weighed a ton at an exclusive fine art publisher's stand. And once in the past I'd read a few fairy tales, although I can't for the life of me remember whether they were originally Indian or just generally Oriental. In short, my curiosity had been piqued, and I nodded emphatically. The fair organizer closed his mouth and enclosed me in his powerful arms, only for a few seconds, but it felt like an eternity to me.'

'I happened to be carrying around with me a slim short story that would be easy to translate. In substance, it was the life of the grand-mother of a girl I went to school with in Lübeck, one of those stories you never forget. And it was this unpublished tale that I'd written down a couple of months before the book fair, condensing it into a short story, and had even asked my editor to look at it, as if I'd antici-pated that it might soon come in handy.

'The heroine of the story . . . I threw it away one day like all the other unpublished pieces I've penned, as people say, even if no one writes with a pen now; but maybe it's still lying around somewhere, the English version at least.

'Anyway, the heroine of this story, my version of which no longer exists, was a simple, industrious woman who mended clothes and whom I'd simply called the *seamstress*, leaving her otherwise nameless. Like my friend's grandmother, this seamstress dreamt her whole life

long of taking the train, just once but as far as possible. After squirrel-
ling away every extra penny for her trip, the woman eventually
bought herself a ticket for her 70th birthday and took a train for a
destination that was very far away—and of absolutely no importance
to her because . . . the journey is its own reward.

'As she sensed all too soon, however, the journey that had
inspired her for so many years was not as wonderful an experience
as she'd hoped. And when her expected bliss failed to materialize, she
realized that reality stood no chance of satisfying her mounting
yearning—as little chance as a real mango, even the ripest, juiciest,
sweetest mango in the world, can live up to someone's conception of
its aroma before fulfilling their wish to taste the fruit.

'My story ended with the bitterly disappointed old seamstress
standing up and walking off the train while it was rounding a bend
between stations at about 30 kilometres per hour.'

'This ought to go quite smoothly, this after-fair event, I thought, set-
ting out on foot towards the Hotel Steigenberger where the head of
programming, or whatever he was, had obviously, before I'd even said
yes, booked rooms not just for the Indians but also for me and
reserved a table for a first dinner with all the participants. The Indian
writers, I thought, would eat a few vegetarian nibbles and then retire
to do some praying or meditation.

'I could not have been more wrong. The Indians—two women,
a tall, fat one and a smaller, twig-like one, and five lusty men—scoffed
their food as if they, as authors, had to prove to all the other guests
and waiters in this chic restaurant that many people in their country
are undernourished and very, very hungry. They ordered salmon and
goulash soup and Wiener schnitzel, followed by chocolate tart and
an espresso, and washed it all down with soda water and large

quantities of the finest scotch, a bottle of which they wished to have delivered to each room. And our host entertained them as if this were a wedding reception. It was getting later and later, my English wasn't particularly good back then and I could make neither head nor tail of their very peculiar-sounding Indian English. I was dog-tired, but the Indian men—the women had slipped away—grew increasingly chirpy. And when one of them got up, probably to go to the toilet, the others put their heads together. It looked and sounded as if they were bitching about the man during his brief absence, not in English but in a vernacular that might have been Hindi. No, I didn't like those Indians; and I was tired of the amateur rocker dressed like Mr Armani, who signed off on all of this with the meekest of smiles and, at the very end, on the massive bill with his Montblanc fountain pen.'

'The next morning, after a hurried breakfast together, we met around ten o'clock, as agreed, on the seventh floor of the Holiday Inn Hotel near Frankfurt's central station. The self-appointed moderator and I were the first ones there, on time, but the others soon arrived in dribs and drabs.

'The fat Indian woman, who, as our moderator announced, had already written over 50 novels, was wearing a fine, ink-blue woollen trouser suit and enormous double gold creole hoops in earlobes that looked worn out by the jewellery's weight. Hanging loosely around the thin Indian woman with the red bindi on her forehead, who must have been slightly older than the fat woman, was a traditional robe with a paisley pattern embroidered on a shimmering blue-green background the colour of a dung beetle's chitinous carapace, a kind of evening gown, only more shapeless and calf-length. She, our moderator said, lived in Bombay and was a successful prose author and playwright as well as being extraordinarily courageous, militant and politically active. Next he presented me and then the five men,

39

who wore aggrieved scowls on their faces, probably because they had had to wait so long. He lauded them—my English was good enough to understand that much—as very well-known authors in India, little of whose work, "for incomprehensible reasons", he stressed, had been published in German. And at the end of his introduction he again lamented that he'd been unable to persuade any German writers other than me, because they had already been on their way home yesterday evening as he was trying to drum together this gathering at literally the very last minute.

'Following the Indians' prose samples and poems, either written in English or translated into English and mostly read out by our moderator, was hard enough because I understood too little and because, being my arrogant former self, I found them either too florid or simply trite, but it was impossible for me to keep up with the discussion, which soon developed into a heated argument. More and more frequently, the two women and the five men reverted from the agreed English to Hindi or some other regional language, and even our moderator, well versed though he was in Indian affairs, completely lost the thread. The men, or to be precise four of the men, totally disagreed with one another on every subject. Their two female colleagues attacked or, rather, boycotted them. Eventually it proved beyond even the bearded old Sikh, whose presumably never-cut hair was concealed under an impressive yellow turban and who'd tried hard to keep the debate factual and calm, to finish a single sentence; one or other of the two Indian women would interrupt him, often not even verbally but by bursting into gales of laughter, the thin one shrilly, the fat one emitting a dull thundering noise like a kettle drum. The women's mirth didn't appear to have been triggered by something one of the men had said, though. It was something else— defensive derision, I think, or naked contempt.

'Speaking of naked: the moment came when something completely unexpected occurred, something monstrous, something that made a lasting impression on me. The thin Indian woman jumped up, turned her back to the speakers and the audience, lifted up her dress under which she wasn't wearing any knickers and wiggled her narrow but still remarkably pert backside like a duck. After no more than 20 seconds she dropped the hem of her dress, performed a military-style about-turn, sat down and smiled as if nothing had happened.

'One of the male contingent was a squat, almost cuboid man whose trouser legs were far too short and who was suspiciously quiet, as far as possible avoiding any eye contact; the only one he occasionally eyed up was me, although only when he suspected I wouldn't notice. Remarkably, it was he who was to blame for the situation escalating. The two women got involved, or at least this is how I interpreted it, in a contest to see who could shock their colleagues the most. The thin woman's performance, that is her wordless, yet unequivocally critical commentary on the entire preceding dispute, had barely finished when the fat, gold-bedecked bestselling author, whose name, Shamim, I shall remember for as long as I live, reached for the shy poet's water glass, grabbed it, drained it in one gulp and slammed it back down on the table.

'At first there was silence. The men froze, totally aghast; and a patch of cold sores broke out so rapidly on the top lip of one, a smart, clean-shaven man in a pressed beige linen jacket, that you could actually see them growing. At first I had no idea what was going on either, but my eyes were like saucers, more from fascination than anything else. These two Indians, I thought, are true feminists, ferocious and audacious fighters, whereas our own feminists spend their time squabbling over suffixes.'

'During what he felt was a necessary break, our moderator, the bloke from the fair whose name has slipped my mind like the names of all the other people sitting there, with one exception, told me that the shy, stout man was an Untouchable, a pariah; they called themselves Dalits, he said, a term derived from a Sanskrit word that meant something like "the downtrodden". The provocative act Shamim had committed not only shattered a general Indian taboo but was also an insult to this Dalit poet. She, Shamim, who was incidentally a member of the second-highest caste, the Kshatriya, had exploited and practically abused him; "but I don't know what for or what against," he added.

'We were served coffee, tea and biscuits but no whisky or wine, even though, judging by their gestures, the Indians definitely needed some alcohol to calm themselves down. The amateur rocker too was aggrieved that we couldn't even order drinks at our own expense.

'The half-hour break eventually came to an end and it was my turn. Our moderator sheepishly but proudly announced that he had translated my short story into English himself. No sooner had he finished reading it than there was another completely unexpected turn of events. The two women gave me a standing ovation, whereas all the men apart from the moderator sat on their hands. The only words I could make out of the torrent that Shamim, still standing and perhaps directing her flickering gaze at nirvana, poured forth like a flaming geyser were "Singer sewing machine" and "very important for Indian woman".

'It was my story that had inspired Shamim to this tirade, I told the moderator, and so this time I wanted a full and literal translation, with, if possible, a few enlightening explanations.

'He obliged me. In India the Singer, as it was almost affection-
ately known, was *the* symbol of women's emancipation. Many poor
Indian women dreamed of owning a sewing machine because the
income generated by homemade quilts, bags, skirts and trousers
enabled them to feed themselves and their children. Many an Indian
woman, Shamim declared, would gladly swap places with the heroine
of my short story, but she would never be so stupid as to chuck her
hard-earned cash out of a train window. Nevertheless, she was sure
that every desperate woman in her country would understand this
story, including my heroine's desire to get away. And therefore, if she
could rustle up the necessary rupees to pay for a flight, she wished
to invite Miss Schröder, meaning me, to Calcutta.

'I was overjoyed by her praise. I would love to visit the teeming
city of Calcutta one day, I replied, and pushed my business card across
the table to Shamim.

'The conversation between the Indians, who had somehow, even
without whisky, managed to compose themselves during the break,
meandered from that point on; all the tension was gone, which might
also have been because the two women treated their fellow
countrymen as such. And then, at long last, our moderator thanked
everyone—officially, on behalf of all the organizers, exhibitors and
guests of this year's book fair this time—and invited his "dear Indian
friends" to a farewell dinner at the Frankfurter Hof hotel. However,
the people for whom he had organized this entire event offered *him*
not a word of thanks, only gracious smiles to signal that they would
welcome an opportunity for further wining and dining.

'I didn't attend that final dinner, even though presumably no one
would have objected and I was keen to talk to the Indian ladies alone,
woman to women; but my English simply wasn't yet good enough to
conduct a proper conversation.

'Exhausted from hours of strained listening, I staggered back to the Hotel Steigenberger, kicked off my pumps, lay down on the bed and immediately fell asleep.

'The next morning, after a filling and luckily lonely breakfast, I went to the station and bought a ticket.

'When the 10:00 train set off north after a 40-minute delay, I felt completely empty, as empty as the compartment in which I was sitting, as empty as the old seamstress in the last chapter of my story.'

'One day in the middle of March the following year, 1987, when I'd almost forgotten that meeting in Frankfurt, I went to my front door to accept a registered delivery, an envelope plastered with plenty of pretty stamps. I didn't slit it open right away, however, because I was suffering from another painful bout of lovesickness. It was only that evening, when I turned the letter over and saw that it was from Shamim that I set about deciphering the one typed sheet with the help of my English dictionary. I was, Shamim requested—no, demanded—, to buy a cheap ticket, fly to Calcutta in May to see them and stay for four days, only four days unfortunately. She could divert a certain amount from the UN's annual grant to her League for Free Indian Women and it would be just enough to reimburse me for the cost of a bargain flight and to cover the hotel expenses, but it wouldn't stretch to more than four nights. She would pick me up at the airport in person and make all the other arrangements. All I needed to do at the planned event was read a few lines in German, just the first paragraph of my short story about the old seamstress and only because my language sounded so unfamiliar to Indian ears. She would then make sure that the entire story got a hearing, either in the English version or, if she were capable of translating it, in Hindi. And she also wanted to have a brief conversation with me after the reading. Admittedly, my English wasn't up to much, but I did have a few weeks to practise. She sent her regards, Shamim wrote at the end of her letter, and was sure I would accept. She needed to know my arrival time as soon as possible. I was to send a telegram or call her.

'Next to Shamim's ornate signature, in large, clear letters that might have been written by a school kid, were another address, probably her League's, and four different telephone numbers.'

'I don't know what it was about fat Shamim, what the whole deal with her had been since the beginning, but I saw no prospect of defying her wishes—orders, more like—let alone turning her down. Four days in Calcutta . . . One glance at the atlas sufficed for even me to understand that this giant in India's far east was *the* mole on the arse-end of the world. I would be in mid-air for an eternity to get there and I didn't like flying; also, after many months with a broken heart, I could hardly have been feeling less enterprising.

'All the same, I went the next day to a travel agency in the centre of Lübeck, where I was living at the time, and learned that if I agreed to take the cheapest option, the one with three stopovers each way, one in Frankfurt, one in Paris and one in Bombay, costing the paltry sum of 1,400 marks, it wouldn't take an eternity, not even half an eternity, oh no, just a piffling 22 hours there and 26 hours back. Although I'd barely 3,000 marks in my account and Shamim had written that I'd be reimbursed for the flight expenses—only, who knew when—I decided not to pass up but instead to snap up this offer, which the young woman at the counter of the travel agency regarded as a bargain and unbeatably cheap on such a shoestring budget, and, provoked by this bimbo's arrogant attitude, I waved my credit card with exaggerated nonchalance.'

'Maybe I should have rung Calcutta before I did this, since Shamim transferred me, albeit half a year after I got home, only two-thirds of my advance because, as she explained in great detail when we parted, there must have been an even cheaper option. The fact that I would in that case have travelled for something like 60 hours was of no further interest to her; after all, the white blackamoor had served her purpose by then . . . '

'On arrival I was wiped out after virtually a whole, sleepless day of sitting in the middle seats of a jumbo jet and two smaller planes, surviving on stingy on-board meals, waiting in poorly ventilated transit lounges and queuing for passport control. Cunningly, I only had hand luggage, and luckily I spotted Shamim straight away, bobbing above the crowd on the other side of the swinging exit door like a buoy on the surf.

'We didn't hug, just shook hands, which was a moist, indeed a wet business because the heat in the arrivals hall of this international airport with the peculiar name of Dum Dum was unbearable. It was breathtakingly humid out in the open too, but it was hardly 'out in the open' because we had to fight our way through a teeming swarm of people the like of which I had never seen until Shamim, who was wearing a sky-blue silk sari with her gold creole hoops this time, bundled me and my small wheeled suitcase into the back seat of a Mercedes taxi fit for the scrap heap and got in next to the driver.

'After about two hours' crawling along between cars that honked their horns incessantly for absolutely no reason, past cows and sheep, crooked huts, pedestrians balancing a variety of items on their heads, and women, men and children sitting or even lying on the pavement, we must have been approaching the actual city because some tall stone buildings loomed on the hazy horizon beyond a broad band of neon signs, billboards, fashion stores, supermarkets, cookshops, shacks and piles of goods. Soon, very soon, I thought, we would reach the hotel where Shamim had hopefully booked me an air-conditioned room. There I could gather my wits, have a shower, sleep . . . But whenever we weren't stuck in traffic, we kept driving, on and on, and at Shamim's behest we wound up the windows to keep out the all-pervading stench or because she was afraid of thieves. The houses and huts we crawled past became ever smaller and shabbier, the animals, which now included dogs, goats, chickens and even monkeys, grew in number and the humans grew more and more raggedy-looking. Finally, however, we stopped outside a corrugated-iron hut, surrounded by a number of sparsely foliated, dusty trees, in a slum whose centre this hut may have marked.

' "Come on, we don't have much time," hissed Shamim, boring between two and four of her manicured sausage fingers, tipped with long nails varnished a fiery red, into my back.

'And then I saw images that still haunt me in a recurring night-mare from which I awake every time in tears, since, strictly speaking, it is not a dream but a trauma, a reminder of the worst sight on which I have ever laid eyes; and Lord knows our job provides its fair share of horrors. But compared with this hole—or rather, hell—near Calcutta, Dante Alighieri's evocation is but a nursery rhyme.

'Inside that unexpectedly spacious corrugated-iron hut, which was windowless and therefore artificially and not particularly brightly lit, two or maybe three hundred women sat densely packed on folding chairs, their faces—no, their features—horribly deformed. Sure, not every one of those overwhelmingly skinny figures of indefinable age was equally mutilated, but none was unscathed. As we entered, crippled and fingerless hands waved to us. Some of the women no longer had noses, others had lost an eye or an ear—or both of both. Others still had disfigured, rubbery lips, some had none at all—no teeth either, leaving their mouths like permanently gaping holes. One woman in the front row had hardened lines of scars that tugged the corners of her mouth apart and upwards, and her frozen grin left her two remaining canines bare, like a cartoon Dracula. And sclerotic contractures had pulled the hairless head of the woman next to her askew and askance; it was wedged in a grotesquely twisted pose between her shoulders, and every time she tried to look up, she was racked with gruesome groans.

'Whether there were other deformities, on the women's bodies for instance, I could not tell. The women weren't naked but wrapped in lengths of fabric; it was as if they were pupating in their saris, like caterpillars or mummies.

'And rather than anything or anyone else there, it was these butterfly-bright or widow-white saris, concealing everything but heads, hands and feet, that seemed to taunt me and caused the crock of tears I was literally to overflow. Shamim, the *grande dame* of this bizarre community, had long since spoken a few words of introduction and dug her elbow into my ribs repeatedly to get me to start reading at last. But I remained silent and still: despite Shamim's nudges, the "compassionate German guest", meaning me, was slumped in a creaking basket chair, lifeless and weeping. Tears were streaming from my eyes as if my insides had completely liquefied and were now rising unstoppably to the rims of my eyelids, over which I was powerless to prevent them spilling. At least my nose wasn't running yet, and I still had my clenched lips under control, which is precisely why I had to keep my mouth shut, however demandingly and increasingly roughly Shamim rammed her elbow into my side. Obviously I wanted to get a grip of myself, but the harder I tried, the harder I cried. Was it because I felt so surprised?

Was I weak from the heat, from thirst and hunger? Or was it a mixture of my long repressed and suppressed lovesickness and the strain of my journey? It was probably all of those things combined, that is self-pity and not, I knew then and know today with utter certainty, pity for those spectral women.

'Soon they took pity on *me*, though. Some of them got up, approached me, ran their hands over my hair, patted my clenched fists, muttered some friendly-sounding words and scattered sugary sweets and peanuts on the manuscript before me, which looked as if I'd left it out in the rain. That did nothing to improve my plight, though. Oh no, those attempts to comfort me, by those women of all people, were unwelcome. Worse: they were embarrassing. The wailing shook me like a wet dog shakes itself. I sobbed and sniffed and was incapable of even getting to my feet and stepping outside to those dusty trees in whose sparse shade I might potentially have regained my composure; I simply couldn't stand up.

'And so I just sat there, still desperately trying to control my tears.

'Once, I thought that I was okay again, that I might gradually calm down if I could shut my eyes or stare only at the ceiling, but then a horrible hiccup suddenly rattled me, and I fought it as unsuccessfully as I had my compulsive weeping. —I was defenceless; believe me, never ever, even during puberty, which was truly a dark age, have I felt so defenceless.

'Shamim must have had enough at some point; she said something, I couldn't understand what, and began to declaim my story, in Hindi I guess, and in a pretty impassioned manner, I felt, and her powerful voice drowned out my own siren wail, which was in fact subsiding now—the two were probably linked—, and its syncopating hiccups.

'When she finished reading, there was a surge of applause that lasted for several minutes. The women just kept clapping, on their feet and even as they left the hut. "Shamim, Shamim, Tamara, Tamara," they chanted, emitting strange, canary-like trills.

'And eventually Shamim's hot mitt reached for my arm. She pulled me out of my basket chair and slipped her arm through mine; we were practically the last to leave the hut and we got back into the taxi, which had come back or been waiting for us.

'This time, however, Shamim didn't get in beside the driver but next to me; and once again she drove the left one of her unbelievably pointy elbows into my soft tissue, but this time, to my not inconsiderable surprise, she did so as encouragement, with enthusiasm.

' "Marvellous," she cried. "That was absolutely marvellous! Our brave women will never forget you. No one has ever wept for them before, what's more a stranger, a foreigner. Your tears, Tamara, were like morning dew on wilting summer roses to them."

'Of course, Shamim said all this in her odd Indian English, which now that I was reliant on her, I was finding easier and easier to understand.

'And as we drove along or waited in another traffic jam, Shamim told me something of which I'd had not even an inkling of an idea, namely that those women had been attacked with cooking fuel. There were apparently thousands of them, in every corner of India.

' "Many of them," Shamim said, "sooner or later die of their burns. But those in the audience just now were lucky or unlucky enough—some see it one way, others differently—to have escaped with their lives. Mothers-in-law are the main culprits; they commit most of these crimes, and our laws carry harsh punishments for them *if*, I said *if*, someone is brave enough to report them and if a judge is willing to press charges and initiate legal proceedings. But even in those cases there's rarely any tangible evidence. It's usually the word of one badly injured woman against that of her entire village; and in the end the old witches stride out of the courtroom victorious." '

'Later, back home, I read every book, every article and anything else I could borrow from libraries and via inter-library loans about a topic that was not as popular then as it is now. The tears I'd shed during my real-life encounter with these partially burnt women didn't return as I read, but I was sick to my stomach. One time, I spent at least an hour with my head over the toilet bowl in the ladies' lavatories of Lübeck central library and felt as if it wasn't just my breakfast I needed to throw up but everything I'd ever eaten or drunk, even the amniotic fluid my grandma had told me I'd almost choked on at birth.

'The sole reason for these attacks is the dowry the bridegroom and his clan expect and receive from the bride's parents; if it's not high enough, perhaps because the bride's family is poor and has further daughters to marry off, it is grumpily accepted at first. But after the wedding, as extravagant as possible and also paid for by the bride's parents of course, the husband's kin are bound to return with fresh demands and often specious arguments. The young woman, who of course lives with them now, is lazy and clumsy, they carp, eats too much and has presented them—this is the clincher—with a first-born daughter rather than the expected son. Such a start bodes ill for the future.

'An Indian saying goes: "Raising a daughter is like watering your neighbour's garden."

'But the parents of the unfortunate woman—let's call her Nala— who have already gone into debt to pay for the dowry and the wedding, are either unable or unwilling to be blackmailed until the end of time, pouring more and more money into the maws of a gang of greedy in-laws.

'So how does this gang solve a problem that's becoming a real headache for them, especially considering they too might have two or three girls sitting around at home and have sold off their only son so hastily and so cheaply? Very easily. One day Nala is standing in the kitchen, bending over the onions she's chopping, and behind her, next to the kerosene stove, stands her mother-in-law. It only takes one little push: Nala's cotton or even nylon sari, her back, her hair, her face and her chest catch fire and, before you know it, the entire woman is ablaze. And none of these monsters hostile to Nala will attempt to put out the flames, not even her husband's kid sisters who will probably soon be dealt equally awful cards themselves.

'When the young woman succumbs to her injuries, ideally without delay, though she often first has to endure days or even weeks of indescribable torment, the case is closed, for everyone, not least the cash-strapped or perhaps merely stingy parents of the bride who, for fear of malicious gossip, would never ever have taken their daughter back or else, at a pinch, their little granddaughter. The murder is declared a regrettable accident, and the widower is free to marry the next dead woman walking, and his clan is free to collect the next dowry.

'Dowry, a peculiar word, one that, now I know about these things, has a slightly Indian ring to it.

'If, however, she doesn't die—maybe there wasn't enough fuel in the stove or else she managed to run out of the house in flames into a fortuitous downpour—this blundering Nala or Asha or Sunita is cast out. No man is obliged to keep such a hideously disfigured wife, unfit for his bed or to do the housework; let her take her brat, it's only a girl anyway, and clear off.'

'It was in similar terms, well, perhaps not in quite such detail, that Shamim spoke about these Indian women's martyrdom during the drive back to central Calcutta and then, even before we reached my hotel in Tangra, one of Calcutta's many shanty towns, she told me the true reason for her invitation.

' "Now," she said, "you are in the picture and you even wept with emotion. And so you must clearly see what we really need more urgently than your tears. The only hope for my protégées are sewing machines, lots of sewing machines; as soon as they have those, they will be able, with the help of our organization and yours of course, to set up cooperatives. Groups of between five and ten women will share two to three machines and take out a small loan for fabric and other materials, providing of course that they already own the most important thing, the sewing machines; they serve as collateral, because if the repayments don't work out, then even second-hand ones can be sold on at a profit in India. Your mission now, Tamara, is to procure these sewing machines; about 100, or better 200, will be enough for starters, the model and the supplier don't matter, but they have to be free, and the transport mustn't cost us anything either. You can manage that, can't you?"

'Shamim's "can't you?" sounded less like a question and more as if it would be a scandal, an indelible stain, if I were to fail.

'I spent the next day and the day after that with the rat-a-tat of a sewing machine ringing in my head. *One*? Rubbish —hundreds! Most of the time I dozed on my hotel bed beneath the decrepit ceiling fan, unable to think, see and hear anything but sewing machines, sewing machines, sewing machines . . . In fact, I was almost glad, because those sewing machines and Shamim's instructions, to which I hadn't dared to raise the slightest objection, rather effectively displaced the images of those women's devastated faces.'

'I'd asked Shamim not to arrange any events for me and she obviously hadn't even planned anything. "You're a grown woman," she said. "Look around. And pay attention to things you probably find repulsive. And you have my phone numbers if there's any problem." '

'I only went for one short walk, however, and it wasn't a proper one because it was boiling hot, because child beggars assailed me at every corner and because I soon couldn't figure out where to put my feet to avoid tripping over people lying here and there. No, I didn't go shopping for little bracelets, earrings or silk fabrics, and only occasionally fetched a pot of dal and a cardboard bowlful of rice with spicy vegetable mush from the stall next-door to the hotel. But I can safely pass over such details; they're unimportant. We've both seen enough clichés, misery and bad fast food.'

'Since I was already in Calcutta, I'd actually planned to visit Nirmal Hriday, the hospice for the dying founded by Mother Teresa, who was still working there in person, at least on and off, when she wasn't travelling the world—for purely missionary reasons, of course. However, after what I'd seen in that hut and been unable to stomach, I felt so listless that even the idea of getting there was terrifying. Maybe I was afraid that my guilty conscience might entice me to stay in Kalighat for a while as one of the many volunteers lending a hand to Mother Teresa's Missionaries of Charity. And I had to get home as soon as possible to start the sewing-machine campaign whose necessity—in the most literal sense—Shamim's shock tactics, actually a form of brainwashing, had made clear to me, no, rammed down my throat.

'So I just lay there on the hotel bed, thinking not about the city I found myself in but about how I might be able to get in touch with the Singer office in Germany and whom and with what kinds of letters I might ask for help—PEN and the Writers' Union, two societies of which I was not a member, and the editors of the women's magazine EMMA, which might perhaps print an appeal for donations. I wondered if any German firms manufactured sewing machines and whether I shouldn't place adverts in the two largest national newspapers at my own expense and whether that would cost me dear and whether it wasn't in fact transport that would be the biggest financial problem. After all, sewing machines, even the smaller, lighter portable ones, are not calculators.'

'On the evening of the third day, the night before my return flight, Shamim came to my hotel as promised. When she gave a quick rap, entered and stood in the doorway with her arms crossed, leaving the door open of course, I was still lying on my bed, as I had nothing but sewing machines in my mind, not even our appointment. Under Shamim's impatient gaze I got up, slipped into a skirt, T-shirt and sandals and was ready in a flash. I almost saluted: Tamara ready to go out!

'We took a rickshaw, but for only about an hour this time, to a restaurant which, Shamim explained with a smug grin, belonged to her organization and was run by five ex-prostitutes; it was pretty successful, she said, and was even making a profit already because it served the best meat and two veg, Mughlai-style.'

Meat and two veg, Tamara had said, although Shamim surely hadn't because it's a typical term for traditional fare—but also for the male genitals. And the context in which Tamara used it leaves a bad taste in my mouth.

'Shamim,' Tamara continued, 'ordered something, I forget what, handed me a file containing information and again impressed upon me their urgent need for the sewing machines, at least 150 of them. I should tell people in my rich homeland about the disfigured and outcast women and definitely write about them, she said, and then many more people would surely be willing to support the projects of her League for Free Indian Women.

'No word of friendship for me, no enquiry about how I was feeling or at the very least about my impressions of Calcutta; ever since that first meeting in Frankfurt, Shamim had obviously been intent on exploiting me—like the short Dalit poet whose glass she had drunk from. My short story and I had been no more than a means to an end for her. But I didn't really hold it against her, especially as she made no attempt to conceal her true objectives. On the contrary: I admired her coolness, her willpower, her single-mindedness. In order to offer those women, who had literally been through hell, a halfway bearable future, Shamim seized every opportunity that arose with no regard for lost illusions, let alone a single, sensitive German writer's soul.'

'And that was exactly how our leave taking at Dum Dum airport played out—more businesslike than warm. Shamim did however give my hands, which were soaking from my fear of flying, a good press, but only after lecturing me on the subject of my excessive travel expenses and having the effrontery to remind me once more of our "shared mission".'

'As you can imagine, as soon as I got back to Lübeck I devoted myself to the campaign I named "Sewing Machines for the Women of India"; forgotten or forgone were my chronic lovesickness and the struggle with my next novel, which remained a fragment and disappeared years ago anyway. I published appeals for donations, two of which I paid for myself, and one that EMMA printed free of charge, wrote to the German representatives of Singer Sewing and Embroidery Machines, to PEN, to the German Writer's Union, the German manufacturers Pfaff, Dürkopp-Adler, Seidel & Naumann, Kunze AG, Maier, Kannegiesser and others I had tracked down. As I didn't have the patience to wait for replies, I phoned lobbyists, managers and spokespeople for these companies and institutions, describing my experiences, arguing, cajoling, beseeching and begging.'

'I must have been highly persuasive because after eight weeks or so I'd received pledges of 130 sewing machines, mostly discontinued models that would normally have been flogged off or gone unsold. And in my flat I stored a further 44 travel and portable sewing machines—others I turned down for lack of space—along with various spare parts, yarn, tailoring tools and cash donations that strangers transferred, sent by post or sometimes even brought round. The transport costs, which were indeed humongous, were covered by PEN and the Ministry for Health, Women and Social Affairs. The sewing machines, all 174 of them, were delivered to the League's address. In some cases, it was the companies themselves that arranged the transport; otherwise, it took place only after PEN or the ministry had transferred the corresponding funds. I used the monetary donations, which eventually came to around 4,000 marks, to cover the shipping of the machines and spare parts that had accumulated in my home.

'I didn't hear anything from Shamim for a long time; she never rang me. —Still, a good half a year after our goodbyes at Dum Dum airport, one final, brief letter arrived, in which she informed me that 13 cooperatives had been established. She owed me thanks, it said below two or three terse lines, not from her but on behalf of the "forgotten women" of her city.'

'Oh Asta, I was as proud as punch of what I'd achieved as well as exhausted and through with everything. Writing, that was clear to me now, would neither satisfy nor feed me in the future. So I drew the only trump card I'd ever been dealt from my sleeve, not the ace of spades but at least the ace of diamonds—the wonderful profession I'd been trained to do and which I could practise again wherever, whenever and for as long as I wanted. And that, Asta, is why I'm sitting here today, with you, in this deep, dark, Romanian hole.'

Hang on a second: is it possible that old Asta Arnold remembers verbatim what Tamara told her years ago, all the dates and troubles that befell Tamara Bunke, a long-forgotten, now rotten, minor icon of a revolution which is over again or still, and little more than prehistoric pop art to the children's children of those she once incited? And did that stuff about the Indian women really come from Tamara? Or does Asta know about it from books, newspapers or TV reports? Does, or did, Tamara Schröder even exist? Definitely? Probably? Maybe? Assuming she exists or did exist, for she might not even be alive now, is or was she similar in character to the woman Asta saw at the supermarket till or even believes she recognized? And if Asta really did meet Tamara, did that woman write a novel, meet a Shamim and visit Calcutta? Or are Tamara and Shamim and their stories invented? Or half real and half invented? And what was that about Asta's old friend Carmen and the North Korean cook whom she allegedly picked up back in the days of the GDR?

In the Munich Airport compound, odd people heave into Asta's view, acting as a cue or inspiration for her memory or her imagination or this ominous yet fairly manipulative inner voice, or a mixture of all three. She believes she's merely remembering, and she's not in the least surprised that these memories, or what she takes for memories, turn out to be so vivid, yes so overflowing with detail. So? Is she glad at least? No, she accepts it as something completely normal. She believes she must be a kind of elephant and as those creatures are said to do, her brain even seems to have permanently registered things from long ago, not every word she ever heard or read of course, but sounds, smells, colours, faces, situations . . .

But if that were true, why does she often fail to do important, even vital things? Why did she inject a patient, whom she admittedly didn't particularly like, intravenously with a serum that ought to have been administered intramuscularly? Why did she repeatedly put medicines in the wrong place, mix up procedures and forget who was on the duty roster and when? Such events and incidents occurred often enough. One even endangered her—and had consequences.

'In spite of a relatively fresh burn on her left thumb, Nurse Asta Arnold used a pair of unsterilized nail scissors, without rubber gloves, to remove necrotic tissue from a large decubitus ulcer, putting both the patient and herself at risk of sepsis. More and more frequently,' her colleagues continued in their two-page request for disciplinary action to the head of the Hospital Alemán Nicaragüense, HAN for short, in the capital Managua, 'she abandons the bedsides of the patients she is supposed to wash, feed and re-bandage, and sits around for hours in our common room, chain-smoking and lost in thought, indeed as if she's spaced out.'

'Those sneaky swamp-grubs,' Asta ranted when she finally found out. The person who'd tipped her off that her colleagues had been despicable enough to write such a letter was none other than Nurse Marlis, the only person at HAN who had made no attempt to conceal her animosity towards Asta, even though or perhaps precisely because neither of them was exactly a spring chicken. Since as many people as possible, apart from Asta of course, ranging from ancillaries and nurses right up to the registrars and ward doctors, were meant to sign the thing, it had been passed from hand to hand, giving Marlis the opportunity to copy out some particularly excoriating passages and slip it, folded very tightly, into the pocket of Asta's scrubs after they'd changed five shit-covered sheets in complete silence.

Had the letter not landed on the clinic director's desk after all, or did he ignore it? In any case, the dreaded disciplinary action never came; there was a bit of covert bullying and then, on 23 June 2013, Asta's 65th birthday, a strange surprise. Her wonderful colleagues and their boss had, as the accompanying flowery card said, 'been busy collecting for this flight to Munich', because Asta hadn't been back home for ages, and maybe this 'outing', as they cutely referred to it, might tempt her to take 'well-earned' retirement at last.

'But I'm from Berlin,' a baffled Asta had explained and asked why, if it had to be Munich, she'd only been given an outbound flight. 'Because you'll hopefully understand that this is your ticket home and the money didn't quite stretch to a one-way ticket to Berlin. And besides, you'd have had to change planes again. Anyway, you can also travel on to your beloved Berlin by train,' Marlis had replied with a broad grin; 'and if you still won't consider giving up, then work yourself to death somewhere in Germany or in Eastern Europe, anywhere but here, thanks very much.'

A sta is still peering through the glass front of the airport supermarket, only more sternly now, at the woman at the till who resembles Tamara or perhaps—Asta cannot shake off this suspicion—*is* Tamara, and is quarrelling with her but, typically for Asta, only in her mind.

Don't act so detached, you could have stuck nicely to the full truth and admitted that you did actually go to Saint Teresa of Darkness at Nirmal Hriday and even stayed there for a while. Until you thought better of your promise and ran off to drum up a bunch of scrap sewing machines back home, as you'd been told, you let yourself be summoned to morning prayers by Mummy's Missionaries of Charity and ordered around all day. You were inclined to the pseudo-religious and the paramilitary as it was; remember your weakness for Tamara Bunke or the effect Shamim had on you. As a result, the narrow beds at Nirmal Hriday and the painted numbers on the walls behind them would hardly have bothered you. But bending over those tin tubs for hours, scrubbing cotton saris, tunics, towels and muslin bandages with hard soap and cold tap water, not to mention those practical plastic sheets twice per day, must have been hard graft, of a kind that didn't really live up to our principles of hygiene.

And I can already see the subsequent scenes playing out before me, as if this were the cinema. The pious sisters' eagle eyes scan every corner of Calcutta for the terminally ill, whom they—four sisters, eight arms, eight legs and between them a little heap of misery—sling onto stretchers and then cart off to the hospice, where not all the retrieved doze their way quietly through the day; some, particularly some of the skeletal, sunken-eyed Muslim women, wail and scream, for instance when people like you, that is, people who are completely alien to them and to one another, who often can't even speak English properly, peel them out of their rags, cut off their sole source of pride, their thick, long, yet purportedly lice-ridden hair, and then, as if that were not enough, shave their skulls to the bone. Why didn't you apply those packs of anti-parasite foam to the women, as was usual and effective even then? Because it was hard to wash off with cold water? After all, in your ranks there were and are enough backpackers searching for self-awareness who could have tried it or patiently combed the grey manes free of lice and nits, as well as having enough money to purchase some anti-lice shampoo or at least a few of those old-fashioned lice combs.

I don't want to put Mother Teresa's, her order's and your noses out of joint; I have no right to. The world and Calcutta's poor are grateful to you. From the very beginning, the vile and archaic caste system was immaterial at Nirmal Hriday; the hospice unreservedly accepted any invalid at any time, even those with HIV, however they had got the disease or however advanced it was. You provide food, rice and bean curry till they drop, a little care, aspirin against everything.

Why someone helps—out of omnipotent megalomania or atheistic and humanistic conviction or not-altogether-altruistic Christian compassion in the speculative pursuit of paradise—doesn't matter; for the time being it's enough that they don't look away and do roll up their sleeves. And if they're going to die anyway, of TB, AIDS, cancer or sheer emaciation, then at least let it be on a camp bed with a plastic sheet under their backsides. Oblige—or allow, as the beatified Mother Teresa saw it—someone to suffer pain, like our favourite saviour, only slightly alleviated by aspirin, yet comforted and potentially converted and baptised, literally in the nick of time, and they have a sure-fire ticket to heaven tucked safely in their pockets, even though all earthly possessions are famously banned.

No, I won't call anything into question now, not even the millions in donations that have been flowing into the Mother's order for decades like the water the Brides of Christ are so generous with; others before me have done that.

And you over there, even if you're cashing euros at your conveyor belt, you know nothing. You're not the Pope, not even a ward sister any more, no more than I am.

Ward sister: the term must come from the first nurses, who were generally nuns, sisters of a religious order, and it sounds as if they were all, as if all of us ward sisters, as long as we *practise* our profession—practise: another stupid word—, are kin to all the patients that there have ever been or will ever be on this earth. Yet no one calls the male nurses 'brothers', even though their ancestors or predecessors served, or like the monks at Nirmal Hriday, still serve in a Catholic order; yet though they may call one another brothers, not even they would allow the dying to do so. Even those Nirmal Hriday monks will die one day; everyone does. That is our entire and only kinship!

I don't even want to think about it, but when, like now, there's no avoiding it, to this day it drives me mad, every time. And I insist: wanting to help may be only an innate reflex, but being able to help is at least a temporary triumph over any creature's vulnerability and frailty—in our profession, humans—and a victory over suffering and the disgust that the seriously ill usually provoke in their healthy fellows. The shrill screams of traumatized infants, the madness on the faces of tortured men and raped women, regurgitated rice pudding, runny yellow excrement and flesh wounds crawling with maggots—this list is accurate, though it has the whiff of a sermon about it—are not for amateurs like community-service volunteers, lifeguards, paramedics and other well-meaning but idealistic dilettantes, squeamish to a man or woman, and, for some time now, not for me either. Yes, my colleagues in Managua are completely right: I've done enough helping. The only thing is, I don't know where I should go or want to go. No money, no home, no family, no friends, no options . . .

A sta shakes her head, lights another cigarette and wanders back to the revolving door. There, in the arrivals hall, opposite a row of seats occupied by a large, sleeping, possibly Arab family, she spots the next victim of her projections, a smartly dressed but unhappy-looking man sitting side-saddle on the narrow counter of the deserted information point, staring at his laptop screen; Asta can't see the screen, only the man's well-proportioned half profile, which resembles that of her one true yet unrequited love. Not resembles—looks exactly like: bushy eyebrows beneath a thick mop of dark hair, aquiline nose, narrow mouth, dominant chin, stubble. And like her heartthrob on that distant evening of his greatest triumph, this man is wearing an elegantly crumpled, beige designer linen suit. From the toes of one of his slender, tanned feet dangles a flip-flop likely to join its fallen fellow at any moment.

The person this man looks so amazingly like was called Georg, Georg Golz, and had, as he stressed tongue in cheek, done a fine art degree in Dresden. Asta met him in 1982 when, after losing both her jobs due to a pending application to leave the country, she'd returned to Leipzig and, to earn a bit of money, had posed nude in the drawing studio of the Berlin-Weissensee art school.

I actually dared to do that, thinks Asta, eyeing the liver spots on the back of her left, cigarette-holding hand. Those little freckle-like dots above the bend between her thumb and forefinger, which Nurse Elisabeth had called 'graveyard flowers'—how long have they been there? Without looking herself over any further, let alone pinching herself, Asta can feel how flaccid her once ample bust is, how wobbly and soft her tummy, though at least it's not furrowed with stretch marks; I could still claim, Asta thinks, after a quick check, that I'm capable of pulling my tummy in.

It was a few days before Christmas, and in spite of the iron stove around which we were permitted to stand and pose in the requested positions, the drawing room was bitterly cold; cold—which also applied to the light of the white-blue neon tubes shining down on us from high above—and silent, the silence broken only by the horrible scratching of charcoal on cardboard. No one said a word, and Georg was just as still, and above all—or to be more precise, *in front of* all these students sitting around us—he could hold still, completely still for an hour. I couldn't do that, however hard I tried. It was tough, considerably harder than I'd anticipated. Within minutes all my muscles were aching; my body, which was still strong and supple then, was cramping, and sweat ran from my armpits; from both armpits, strangely enough. What's more, I was roasting only on the stove side, whereas on the side away from the stove I was awfully chilly; whereas my right nipple blossomed rosily and inquisitively, the left one had shrunk to a nub and was much smaller than the other. The unaccustomed standing had made me dizzy. And to fend off the dizzy feeling, I had to move a little from time to time, 'fidgeting', one of the students called it when the hour was up and we, Georg and I, were allowed to get dressed again.

Georg crouched behind the little stove and counted our money, the modelling fee the students would leave on a wooden pedestal according to their mood and current financial situation, and divided up the coins—it was always coins, never notes—into two, I hoped, roughly equal piles. I wandered about, curiously eyeing up what these budding painters and sculptors had put to paper, and was amazed to find that most of the sketches showed me, or at least the contours of a naked woman.

This kind of thing, breasts, curves of any kind, declared a fat girl whose sheet I studied more closely, was—even if Georg had not performed as poorly as I had—easier to draw than muscles and sinews, you know, male toughness.

I don't know if Georg was offended because only five of the 30 or so students had attempted to draw him or if he decided that it was beneath him, a qualified artist and postgrad, to stoop to this level, literally to *bare himself*, but we never posed together again after that December day and the following night.

We'd collected 48 ostmarks, 24 each. And as were still feeling cold, we decided to go for some grog, not in a pub, since that would have been too expensive, but in Georg's studio, which was near the art school on Antonplatz.

Georg did representational art, something that was considered outmoded, indeed conformist at the time. His Asian-influenced, relatively small watercolours showed empty East Berlin streets in the leaden twilight. They were melancholic pictures, with no people or any other creatures in them; the pictures looked distant, accomplished and yet unfinished, as if they'd been sketched in ink from a

68

slowly receding train—or even from memory. In some of these pictures rain was falling or had just fallen. The wet cobblestones reflected the yolk-yellow glimmer of the gas lamps; even the rows of houses had a dual perspective, one vertical and compact, the other horizontal and blurred. I understood, and understand, very little about painting, but I liked what was hanging on the walls and standing in every corner of the studio, which had presumably once been a shop, and I liked the man who'd created them even more. Because he was primarily a watercolourist and because he made our grey, crumbling capital city look like Venice or Vineta, Georg said with affected nonchalance, his friends called him Aquarius. And as it happened, he'd been born in February and on the Baltic coast, in Putbus on the island of Rügen.

George prepared us some grog the way it should be done, with a generous splash of blended rum, a little strong black tea and some sugar cubes. Yet although I even slept at his place after what felt like 20 grogs, nothing came of us—well, no coupling anyway—not even that one time.

We didn't meet up very often before we emigrated to West Berlin, I two months earlier than Georg on 31 August 1983. However, Georg really did mistake the timid admiration I showed him for friendship when I occasionally visited him and when he came to see me once. The thought probably never crossed his mind that I might want more from him than grog and conversations about painting, mostly his own painting. Why should it? After all, I was, as he had seen when we posed together, not particularly attractive, not even when I was still quite young and quite naked.

But then, at the beginning of November if memory serves, came *the* day. Georg's day—and until the next dawn probably the best day of his life, because a large and prestigious gallery in Charlottenburg showed his pictures, maybe *all* his pictures. Even before Georg made it to the other side of the wall, some diplomats from the Federal Republic had smuggled them across the border using 'ant tactics', meaning one by one and in different cars.

I can't recall how many of his pictures were exhibited in that gallery. Maybe one or two hundred? The curator, who wore John Lennon glasses and had his curly hair up in a ponytail, spoke about Georg Golz's oeuvre, and Georg only entered the brightly lit room with the three squeaky clean windows when the curator had already taken the microphone and the floor and, looking around for the artist, beckoned to those who were still outside to come in. With his characteristic knack for choosing the right moment, Georg strode through the doorway and past me without spotting his old friend huddling timidly in her cloud of smoke, pushed aside some of the visitors who'd gathered around the curator and grinned, so confident of success that everyone immediately knew: he's the one! This handsome man is the new star in the West Berlin art firmament.

The curator didn't speak for long before passing the microphone to Georg, who simply said, 'This is my first real opening event, and it would have been unthinkable where I grew up.' These words may perhaps have been interpreted as a thank you, at least by some of his diplomat fans.

The gallery's four or five rooms filled up extraordinarily fast. More and more people arrived, a situation that was probably not entirely unrelated to the fact that the buffet boasted not only the traditional pretzels but also lavishly topped canapés and an apparently endless stock of a very decent Bordeaux, which a group of down-and-outs with eyes only for the bottles served one another without pause or impediment.

Georg didn't drink wine; he'd brought a silvery Russian hip flask with him, from which he took the odd sip as he worked the room in genial yet relaxed fashion. In his not-very-autumnal linen suit, which smacked of understatement and yet also of a summer-sales bargain, and which fitted him as if it had been tailor made without really befitting him, Georg looked as if he were merely playing the part of the East German he really was. —It's an act, I thought. But is he entangling himself in it or disentangling himself from it? There was something annoying about his performance, about the barely perceptible tenseness under his nonchalant posturing, but oddly this worked to his advantage; it wasn't too obvious that he was having trouble pretending he wasn't going to any trouble, and this, as one of the women near me, a lady with her hair up and a pearl necklace, confided in her similarly spruced-up friend, was 'awfully charming'.

Even before the official opening, someone had stuck a red dot beneath 20 or so of the works, which were cheap by today's standards. The diplomats who'd brought Georg's works west and had therefore probably negotiated even lower prices with him, if not with the gallery owner, had presumably been eager to help their latest dissident discovery get off to a good start, and in conjunction with the melancholy appeal of Georg's watercolours, it worked. Within a few hours, practically every picture was marked with a dot and therefore sold. Georg went to great lengths to maintain his cool exterior, but inside, I was certain then and still am, he must have been beside himself with pride and joy.

After midnight, when most of the guests had already left, Georg announced that he needed a beer. Anyone who felt like celebrating with him was welcome to come along.

The after-hours bar he was drawn to was called The Iguana and was only 200 metres away, at the next corner on the right.

This was my chance to draw myself to Georg's attention. I didn't know if in all the excitement he hadn't spotted me or just deliberately ignored me. And as soon as we sat down with a first beer, I managed to catch his eye. Of course it took a moment for him to recognize me and recall the part of his life associated with me, which he had now so brilliantly put behind him, but then he leapt up, threw his arms wide, bent down to me, pulled me close and gave me a hearty, beery kiss on the lips.

He'd never done this before. I was happy, as happy as he was, albeit for different, starkly diverging reasons. I was merely enthused or confused by the kiss; I couldn't handle Georg's sudden success, though, because unlike him I hadn't really settled into this Western world, so alien despite our shared language. I had first got myself signed off work so that I wouldn't immediately have to get a job to pay the bills. But even the doctor, a Saxon who'd crossed the border years ago, a legendary figure in our circles who'd treated virtually every rookie with special indulgence, merely going through the motions that is, and had made out a certificate for me to present to the job centre although I was as fit as a fiddle and then extended it several times, kept asking me if he could 'hire' me as soon as I'd 'got my temporal and spatial bearings a little'.

Georg downed a few 'Fruit Schultheiss' as he called his favourite pilsner and kirsch liqueur line-up and, as his diplomat mates began to yawn, paid the whole tab, without any real competition of course.

He persuaded The Iguana's tired, sullen landlord, who was already wiping the tables, to refill his hip flask and then announced that he wished to take one last quick look at the gallery on his way to the subway station.

It was four o'clock in the morning when we left the bar. The four diplomats, who'd hung in there to the last, disappeared off to Dahlem or various other better parts of the morning-dark and deserted-looking city in individual taxis that someone, probably the landlord, had called especially for them.

Besides me, Georg's only other companion was Irma, a pretty woman with green eyes and full red lips who'd drunk next to nothing but had been making mooneyes at him all evening. We met not a single person and virtually no cars, and if we hadn't heard from a distance, albeit a relatively close distance, these peculiar muffled, pulsating noises, which to my ears sounded more like a lament than a threat, like a whining kid, it would have been completely silent. Despite the lingering darkness we soon realized that something was wrong, but what?

Georg quickened his pace, and the two of us women also speeded up. And then we saw the mess that the wail of the alarm inside the gallery—which seemed to me to be getting quieter and quieter—had already announced.

A huge jagged hole gaped in one of the three panes of glass, the pavement was littered with broken glass and inside, on the white walls of the gallery entrance, which looked strangely brighter than the outside world even though the lights were out, there was nothing—or no longer anything—other than the little cards with a fat red dot alongside the title of the corresponding canvas.

I'll never forget the expression on Georg's face and how it changed in a fraction of a second; an invisible, perhaps superhuman hand erased his previous look of blessed inebriation for ever and replaced it with one of disbelief. Georg stuck his head into the room and stood there—as if paralysed, his eyes dead—no, unseeing. We froze too.

Before we could move again, time expanded, divided only by the rhythm of my heartbeat, or at least that's how I experienced it. After some time Irma stretched out her hand towards Georg but then immediately withdrew it, as if he were electrified and therefore dangerous to touch. Eventually, after who knows how many long minutes, Georg climbed into the room through the hole, snagging one of his trouser legs on a prong of glass before tearing it free again, and the two of us followed him. Every room we charged through— as if through a burning house from which we still hoped to rescue someone—was empty, utterly empty.

And I'll never ever understand why, in that fateful moment, I snuck out on Georg and Irma, whose cigarette glowed in the half-darkness like a glow-worm's rear end. Maybe it somehow dawned on me that in light of what had just happened, the beery kiss and my insignificant self would no longer mean anything to him.

Did I really calculate so coldly to escape that crazy situation? Or was I simply overcome by fear, fear of the suffering of a man who had only minutes previously seemed so enviable and hence desirable? Was my reason for fleeing really that deep-seated cowardice which, in the face of disaster, particularly one that strikes someone you think you like, suddenly sparks and flares, making almost every witness of that disaster run away, as if it were possible to *catch* disaster like a disease or fire? But maybe I wasn't and am not a total chicken but merely suspicious of myself, due to a lack of self-awareness. Low in self-awareness, high in self-hate, now clear off!

Nothing could keep me there, not even my curiosity as to what Georg might do next.

Bit by bit, I learnt how things turned out that morning and the next day, and not from Georg. Yes, someone or perhaps a gang had broken in and stolen all his pictures and with them his entire life so far. Irma, not Georg, had run to a phone box and called the police, who in turn alerted forensics and the gallery owner. Investigations were launched 'into a number of leads', as they say. Yet even weeks and months later, the criminal investigations department still hadn't made any progress. The culprit or culprits remained phantoms and so couldn't be arrested, let alone sentenced.

Although I assumed that it didn't matter a jot to Georg why I'd left him in the lurch that morning, I was too ashamed to even ring and ask him if he needed comfort, support or help. Nevertheless, I did want to be informed, and so I tried to get close to Irma, who had herself become close to Georg. Since he was, as she put it, 'from the other side' and his sudden fall from the pinnacle of triumph really didn't make it easier to be with him, she almost welcomed my caring/probing enquiries, which became blunter and blunter.

'You,' she said, 'are culturally eastern too and you've known him for longer, but hopefully not better.'

Two months later, the flame of Irma's love for Georg had gone out, which came as no surprise to me because she was a woman, a particularly attractive woman, and—like most women when they realize that their affection is no cure—found the miserable man increasingly irritating.

'I've no idea,' she whined, 'what he really wanted. When all that beauty was gone, so suddenly and inexplicably, maybe he wanted me at least as a trophy or as a balm for his wounds?! He took me to bed like a child does its teddy. It was really good at first, only at night, mind you, I mean sexually. It verged on cuddly-toy abuse. It was a way for Georg to numb himself or to let me numb him, and to show himself or me or both of us that even if his sorrow stopped him painting, at least his other brush down still worked. But as soon as he got used to me and my devotion—perhaps even because of that— I no longer mattered to him. They call it the power of habit, and that's precisely why my power as a drug dissolved so fast. But why exactly? It's not as if I'm from Lower Crinchton, Crouchingvale or some other place out in the sticks! Did I eat his art? Am I to blame for World War II or the division of Germany?!'

Then she told me that Georg's early hope that someone or something might shed light on this mysterious art heist had given way to a profound and all-encompassing sense of helplessness.

How on earth can this go on, he must have asked himself after every day he had passed in idleness, like the one before and the one that followed, with ever more nagging doubts about himself and everything that had happened and was still to happen.

'Frankly, Asta,' Irma said during another phone call later on, 'no one and least of all me has the foggiest idea.'

Oh, right, that was and is still the question: how did things turn out for Georg. A few clues, maybe only rumours, reached me while I was still in West Berlin; and even afterwards, when I was no longer living there but had kept and was subletting my small flat, three letters were redirected to me, letters from Irma, who seemed lonelier than I'd ever imagined it was possible for such a beautiful and self-confident woman to be.

Her fourth and last letter was a reply to the only one I'd ever written to her, containing nothing but birthday greetings and my latest contact details. Nonetheless, Irma gave me a very detailed report on Georg.

The police investigation had been shelved without any results, and our poor artist had apparently fallen into a pit of darkest gloom. Alcohol, hash, neglect. He'd nevertheless summoned up the energy to borrow some money and hire a private detective, but even that had been a total failure. After that, he'd taken the advice of his few remaining friends and sought psychological treatment. 'And now,' Irma wrote, 'he's at least stable enough to work a bit again, freelancing as a restorer for collectors his patrons, those diplomats, put him in touch with because they're so terribly sad about what happened.'

When the wall came down and the GDR joined the Federal Republic of Germany and an agency was established to enable former citizens of the now defunct state to look into their files, Georg was apparently one of the first to claim this right. It's only logical, because it must have slowly dawned on him that the Stasi might have been behind the robbery, and now there was a chance to find out where his pictures had been taken—unless they'd long since been destroyed.

However, as my sub-tenant, an old flame of Irma's, told me during a phone conversation we were actually having for other reasons, even this last hope had been dashed. The files of operational case 'Golden Paw', of which there were 14, did not contain the slightest evidence of any events that had taken place after Georg's 'change of residence'—that was the phrase in Western politicalese—, ending instead with the customs stamp on the bottom of his docket, which had remained at the Berlin-Friedrichstrasse border crossing. And that, as I know despite having never requested or viewed my files, was pretty unusual, for dissidents who'd been ransomed or released because their applications had been approved tended to be spied on after leaving for West Germany, and the results of this surveillance continued to be prepared just as meticulously as they had been in East Germany.

The break-in at the gallery in Charlottenburg and the fate of the stolen pictures was therefore still a mystery and perhaps a recurring nightmare for their painter, Georg Golz. Painter? Was Georg still entitled to call himself that? Was he painting still—or again? Or did he stick to fixing works by other artists? Every brushstroke he made must have been a stake through his heart. Might he, years later, have recovered from probably the most disastrous experience of his life and the ultimate disappointment that not even his Stasi files had produced any enlightening information, and have actually started to paint pictures again, out of self-defence in a sense because restoring paintings would otherwise have been the death of him?

And if so, how did he proceed? Did he picture what he'd lost forever and then seek to recreate his best works, reproducing them from memory and copying himself or at least his own style? Or did he start again from scratch, with large formats, abstract, wild and brightly coloured so that, other than the process of painting itself, there was nothing to remind him of his earlier pictures and no one would suspect that the present Georg Golz was identical to the one about whom not even a yellowed exhibition catalogue had survived? Oh yes, that stupid gallery owner in Charlottenburg hadn't printed one. Maybe he'd been short of cash. Or he simply hadn't expected so much interest in a completely unknown East German painter.

Maybe, in returning to art, Georg—whose talent could not after all have simply dried up—had taken a previously unthinkable path.

Was he sculpting now? Had he discovered the joys of photography? Was he weaving tapestries? Did he design and build furniture? Art, I'd once read, was the chance for talented people to become the masters of their dreams, to distance themselves from an experience, however bad, and transform it into something else, occasionally something sublime.

Yet all these late and somewhat random questions concern only the outer parameters of what had befallen Georg, and the answers I give to myself and no one else are purely speculative rather than spectacular, unfortunately. The central question is a different one: how does a person live, mature and grow old with such a crushing story, and, what's more, knowing only half of it? A story? No, an enigma, which can neither be resolved nor simply dissolves, maybe not even when the person himself has long since dissolved. And then what remains of him? Some meagre savings, a sofa, a wardrobe—or, as in my case, nothing but a suitcase full of old clothes, a greasy shoulder bag, a few photos which one can also call pictures, strangely enough . . .

Now come back down here! Irritated and even a little startled because she doesn't know if she has thought this sentence or if her inner voice has pronounced it, silently but tartly as is its wont, Asta lets the match she was about to hold up to her next cigarette burn down to her fingertips. She flicks it away, takes another one from the box and eventually lights up—again without looking, because all her attention is focused on the man who is now closing his laptop, sliding off the information counter and fishing for his fallen flip-flop with his left foot.

So is that Georg or isn't it? Why doesn't she go over and ask him how his life has panned out since, since that life-changing event?

Maybe pretty well, given his crisp tan and the fine threads he's wearing, Asta thinks. Perhaps he turned his back on art and moved into a different sector altogether. Did he metamorphose into a management expert or even an estate agent, or fall into a wealthy woman's lap?

I should look for a public computer inside and then look up Georg Golz—or get up some courage, walk over to him, stand right under his nose, flash him a flirtatious little smile and say, Hello Georg . . . Get up some courage? Say something? I'm finding those things harder and harder to do. What if he doesn't recognize me?

As Asta wrestles with these speculative ideas, the man grabs his laptop, makes his way to the nearest escalator and disappears down towards the lower level from where the long-distance, regional and local trains depart.

A sta is still annoyed at letting that man, the one she believed might be Georg, out of her sight—and also at her reticence to talk to someone, because it's gradually eating away at her confidence—when chance deals her the next cards, albeit quite a sinister hand. But the two figures shrouded in dark-blue burqas, crossing her field of vision now, don't really remind her of playing cards but of two colleagues, experienced nurses with whom she worked for a few weeks one autumn 18 years ago in the A&E ward of Djerba's district hospital.

Why, Asta wonders, do I hardly ever think of my or our patients? Because my contact with them, although it was more physical and intimate in nature, almost never became personal, and not just due to the communication difficulties; they were—as patients, obviously—not exactly *different*, in the sense of distinct. A broken bone is a broken bone; appendicitis is appendicitis. The gall bladder in room three, we say, or the pancreas on the left by the window. People tend to admonish us for this; they say we no longer appreciate the human behind the patient. Oh we do, I could answer, that's exactly who we see, the human, or the human principle. A human was, is and always will be a human; otherwise, medicine would be even harder than it is already.

It's very often children who leave the most lasting impressions; even with festering wounds all over their bodies, they still look more appealing than adults. You bend over them and their big wide eyes look at you like your own children's, whether you have children or not. Each time it excites a certain broodiness, though perhaps only among us female nurses, and you immediately become gentler, friendlier, more anxious. Children, you think, are guiltless; they still have everything ahead of them, including guilt of course. You soon forget the elderly—and not just because they generally snuff it on you anyway. And you only really realize what an old tortoise you are yourself when you're at last in your bed after work but can't get to sleep because you sense the Grim Reaper prowling around, waiting for his chance to snatch you.

It wasn't enough for those two in that Djerba hospital—if I'm not mistaken their names were Helga and Petra—to be ward sisters, so a kind of sisters already; no, they wanted to be real sisters, sisters in the sense of family. They would probably have been happiest if they'd been born as near-identical monozygotic twins. But even nature couldn't stop them from regarding each other as kindred spirits; and they would outwit her too, you'll see, Helga predicted one day outside the back of the clinic where we met for a smoke between shifts.

The rest of us found Helga and Petra's mutual doting absurd because the two of them had little enough in common in terms of character, let alone appearance. But as we witnessed, they changed that just one week later, as best and as simply as they could, possibly inspired by the fact that the patients and even the doctors often mistook us because of the white scrubs we were required to wear on duty, like soldiers in their uniforms.

It was probably Helga who had the brilliant idea and procured the burqas, not some cheap synthetic tack either, no, pitch-black ones made of a light woollen fabric. From then on, not only most Tunisian women but also our two sisters, when off duty, flitted through Djerba like nightshade and thunderclouds. They swore that they would keep it up wherever their next posting might take them. And when we scornfully questioned Helga during one of our cigarette breaks—when, for once, Petra was not around—she explained, in a similarly scornful tone of voice, that there were no religious motives behind their 'burqa trip'. 'No, we haven't converted; it's just for the hell of it. But that can always change,' she added with a laugh.

'Sure,' scoffed a colleague from the Rhineland, for whom this mission in Djerba was her first, 'you're undercover, as spies for German intelligence or the CIA, to earn a little extra. All joking aside, though, it's obvious why you like these opaque full-body condoms so much: you, Helga, are a very attractive woman, and Petra is really pretty ugly.'

'Well-roared, lion tamarind,' Helga replied, her tone already a little more subdued. And then she said that North African men had kept ogling and coming on to her and once she'd only just avoided being raped. In this 'coal sack', though—yes, that's exactly what Helga called the burqa in her own defence—she felt safe. 'When I put this over the top,' she added, 'no one notices me, and in particular I'm not seen as one of the foreign white hospital harlots those bastards are not surprisingly so horny for.'

No sooner said than done: henceforth no one outside the clinic and the nurses' quarters ever saw Helga's regular face, her long, straw-blond hair and her well-proportioned figure again. And the same, luckily, was true of Helga's bosom buddy Petra, who was about fifty and fat with a chest as flat as a pancake, for Petra really took . . . some getting used to, I would say. She had a short neck, sticky-out ears, sparse grey-brown curls, greasy large-pored skin, piggy eyes, a bulbous nose and a thin-lipped, pallid little mouth that almost disappeared between her chubby cheeks. Why wouldn't she have welcomed Helga's suggestion to walk around Djerba only in a full veil?

Neither of them—they were as thick as thieves—ever again went unshrouded into a restaurant, a bazar or the old cinema that screened at all hours the Arabic-subtitled Bollywood movies Helga was completely addicted to. Also, now that they went around as the *Black Sisters*—as they were aptly nicknamed—not only were they protected from covetous or contemptuous glances, they also attracted the sympathies of most of our patients and local assistants—and even gifts such as embroidered cushion covers, mocha cups with gold ornamentation, plastic flowers, crocheted gloves . . . No further burqas, although Helga and Petra might simply not have shown them to us.

Opposite the revolving door, at the edge of a parched patch of lawn, a black-and-grey-striped cat is sitting among clumps of nettles and dandelions; it has its head tilted and its eyes shut and is behaving as if it could not care less about anything or anyone. Still, Asta feels that the cat has noticed her, even taken notice of her. You cats aren't animals, she thinks, you're beasts, and therefore potentially . . . ? You have three guesses. Correct! If it were to suit evolution's or some higher being's—anything is possible— plans to set you on your hind legs and grow your brains, you'd soon be as good and evil as we humans. Now make yourself scarce, you little scallywag, and don't cause me any trouble; your fellow kitty-cat caused me enough of that with in Tunisia.

Tunisia: I liked the country actually and even went there on vacation once after my assignment in Djerba. 'Vacation': yet another weird word; try to picture it and all I see a big, deep, empty hole. I prefer 'holiday' . . .

Anyway, I went on holiday with Kurt to a beach blighted by concrete blocks in a place called Hammamet. Kurt had booked us a bungalow there, a last-minute deal, because, as he said, 'you always need a bit of adventure in your life'. And bingo! Our bungalow was in the final third of a fenced, no, walled tourist ghetto, a long way from the sea and the giant swimming pool. Fortunately, though, from there, near the boundary with the litter-strewn, steppe-like patch of land that began beyond that wall, at least we couldn't hear the holiday reps bawling 'Hands up, baby, hands up' every evening.

Austrian Kurt, whom I'd met during a congress of European aid organizations in Vienna in 1990, was not some big-spending Vienna-dweller, let alone a big-mouthed, greasy fellow, but rather an ambitious social scientist from Styria who was doing his PhD at Vienna University at the time and was often glued to his desk until late at night, regardless of whether I happened to be visiting or not. So, once we'd been together for a while—actually, *together* isn't quite the right word, since we didn't see each other much—I sometimes called my Styrian *Mr Iron Arse*, but only back home and never to his face.

It was our second holiday together, having spent our first on the Greek island of Lesbos. It was beautiful there—and so peaceful. I only had to squash a few spiders and chase away the geckos, which would definitely have appreciated the spiders, but Kurt was resolutely opposed to this idea. Apart from ants, which on account of their well-organized body politic, as he put it, could be sure of his esteem—as long as they didn't attempt to run across his flat—all non-human creatures were suspect, especially 'proper animals'; he dismissed my objection that there was no such thing as an 'improper animal'. — *Proper* animals, he said, included, with the exception of ants and maybe bees, every species on earth, from whales to mites.

Kurt particularly loathed feathered and furry fauna. He was allergic, 'it was a fact', he said, to birds, horses, dogs and cats, but spiders—and they were present in huge numbers in our accommodation on Lesbos—and emerald-green, button-eyed geckos, which looked as if they were smiling, were horrid, he said. —'Horrid' was one of his favourite words.

Four or five of these charming, timid reptiles lived in the Venetian blind cassette above the window and darted in and out of the two holes for the control cords. At first, but then no longer as it was necessary 'to take steps', they had clung to the ceiling and the walls with their wonderful sticky feet, preferably when it was getting dark, on the lookout for flies, moths and mosquitoes; it was only for that reason and at that time of day that I'd been able to observe them a little more closely.

But Kurt had started whingeing on the third morning of our holiday that he couldn't sleep a wink, either at night or during the day, if he had to fear that one of those geckos, sticky-footed or not, might lose its grip and drop on his face. 'Asta,' he cried, 'get rid of those beasts! You're a nurse. They don't revolt you.'

And wimp that I am, I obeyed and jammed newspaper into both of the holes by the ceiling. And yes, it turned out just as Kurt had wished: not a single gecko showed its face again before we left; and I anxiously hoped that the comical little bunch had found an escape route rather than dying in agony in the prison I'd created for them inside the Venetian blind cassette—and not out of love for Kurt, either ...

When, after the delayed flight from Vienna and the bus journey from Tunis, we reached Hammamet-Yasmine, we were so disappointed by the artificial feel of the entire place and the enclosure where we were set to stay for four weeks, by our bungalow's meagre facilities and the fact that there was no kitchenette, only a dining room with fixed mealtimes, especially as by now we'd missed the evening feeding time, that we simply threw our suitcases on the bed, took a taxi to the harbour and looked for an outdoor table at the nearest restaurant.

'More couscous?' Kurt asked.

'Go ahead and enjoy your puke-puke on your own,' I replied snottily. I considered simply getting up and going somewhere else without him. But I was thirsty, with a phenomenal craving for alcohol, which soon arrived in the form of a carafe of anise-flavoured spirit and every glass had the effect of increasing my belligerence now that the sun was going for a dip and surrendering its power over the sea to the moon and its cheerleaders the stars, although from my seat I could only see that by turning around. Kurt had his back to the pergola and thus a good view. Since there was not even the odd lizard slithering between the clematis tendrils, I, on the other hand, had no choice but to look him in the eye, Kurt, Mr Iron Arse, who was utterly unmoved by my rotten mood and continued to shovel couscous into his mouth.

'Oh, don't make that face. Our refreshing holiday has only just begun,' he said, seeking to appease me. —'Refreshing': this word and other old-fashioned words he used made me, as he very well knew, even angrier, especially as here, even in the evening and near the water, it was not at all refreshing but in fact oppressively muggy.

Kurt liked it warm, hot even; I didn't. When the temperature rises above 28 degrees I feel limp, almost ill. But it was my own fault and, what's more, I'd paid for this trip. 'Go for something cheap!' I'd told Kurt over the phone . . .

In Lesbos we'd split the costs. We'd stayed in a pretty bedsit right by the beach owned by a friendly couple, she a teacher, he an engineer. We'd been able to shop in the village, cook for ourselves and lie in. Despite the business with the geckos, we'd got on well and had sometimes even got close, even though I was barely in love with Kurt any more by then.

Barely in love: that had happened many times before, and it had been enough for me, probably because my greatest fear was lovesickness, something that—other than that one time, with Georg, though I'd probably imagined it all—I had never actually experienced; I'd never managed to face *this* sickness calmly when it struck my friends or colleagues. But the idea of having to experience lovesickness myself, something as serious as the case Tamara had described, scared me out of my wits—and it sends shivers down my spine even now, although for me the game is long since over.

How did things continue that first night? Did we really have an almighty row and split up for a few hours? Did we eventually go back to our kennel behind the wall together? Or each of us alone? By taxi or on foot? I can't remember; I'd even forgotten what Kurt told me— the next day—over lunch; we'd slept through breakfast.

Anyway, the beach lived up to our expectations. It was wide, with white sand, and the sky was a cloudless blue. The sun above us had passed its zenith, and a gentle breeze was blowing off the sea. Kurt lay motionless for the rest of the day like a sheet of brown paper next to our assigned, round, palm-fronded parasol, which we'd found immediately because its number, 356, was identical to our bungalow's, and I sat under it, reading and drinking gallons of piss-warm lemonade to chase away the caterwaul of a hangover I'd traded for the anise drink.

What I couldn't chase away, though, was the actual cat screeching and maltreating the mat outside our hut when we got back from the beach—no matter how worked up Kurt became, as he loudly demanded that steps be taken.

That cat too had a black-and-white-striped coat, like the one over there, which is leaving now, perhaps put out by its fellow feline's arrival in my thoughts. Unlike this airport cat, though, the moggy in Hammamet-Yasmine was heavily pregnant; I'd noticed straight away because the otherwise spindly little thing had an outrageously big tummy.

'Get lost!' Kurt hissed, and for a fraction of a second I wasn't sure whether he meant the cat or me. But it was of course the cat that was meant to clear off—and I was meant to ensure that it did.

'She's hungry,' I said, 'and what's more, she's about to have kittens.'

'What about me?! If you let that stray into our room even once, I'll develop a cold and a rash and have trouble breathing.'

Kurt acted completely hysterically, hopping from one foot to the other, then backwards and calling to the cat, which looked at him in amazement, over his shoulder: 'Shoo! Shoo! Get lost, you evil Fuzzball!'

I liked *Fuzzball*—and I liked the animal too, which at least had a name now, even more. For peace's sake, I grabbed Fuzzball, who didn't resist and even began to purr, and put her down again three bungalows away. Let her try begging there.

After checking that the cat was no longer anywhere near him, Kurt unlocked our cabin and put on a pair of jeans, a fresh shirt and a jacket.

'Wash your hands before touching me, then let's go and eat,' he said so coldly that I had to put on a cardigan.

The rows of aluminium bowls containing salads, vegetables, bits of meat and fish, sauces, boiled potatoes and pasta were cold too, colder in any case than the stuffy air under the neon tubes shining their mercilessly bright light down from the brown coffered ceiling onto the long line of guests queuing for the buffet, and onto the Formica tables with half-naked families around them, talking loudly with and over one another in Dutch and English but mainly in German.

Next to the desserts, if that's what you could call the sludgy puddings and dried-out cream slices, at the point where the buffet ended, a man of about 50, to whom I took an instant liking, stood submissively, peering out both uncertainly and expectantly from under his chef's hat. It was clear that he was responsible for feeding this whole queue and was hoping for a nod, a greeting, a thank you maybe, even if only one mumbled out of politeness. Maybe the man knew his meal was no good and yet was still proud because he'd put his heart into it and had, so to speak, pulled himself up to the full height of his ability. No, he clearly wasn't a master of his art, but passably mediocre, at any rate good enough for the mediocrity it was his job to feed here. And he needed this back-breaking job because when the season was over, he'd be left with none, again. They'd probably only just hired him, and never before had he seen such a mass feeding operation. A guest who didn't simply walk past him or perhaps even whispered a word of praise would help him to stick this out and hopefully impress the hotel manager as well.

So I went over to this head chef after the meal and before the cigarette I thought I desperately needed.

'Your gazpacho and the stuffed peppers were really delicious,' I lied.

Oh how his face lit up at this; it was as if my words had flicked a switch and electricity could finally flow to the little lamps hidden inside his black pupils!

The man might even have believed me, but there was no doubt that he'd understood me because he replied in German, 'Yes, madam, the peppers are an old family secret.'

'Recipe,' I corrected him. 'You mean, a family recipe.'

His response: 'No, secret. I have many secrets.'

This made me laugh for the first time since I'd arrived in this holiday slum. 'Asta,' I said, holding out my hand; 'Imad,' he said, taking it.

That's how my friendship with the Tunisian chef began; it was short and, like most friendships, comparatively painless. Under different circumstances more might have come of it—or less, depending on how you look at it; I consider love to be less. —Chefs, whether good or bad, had something about them that turned me weak at the knees, and unlike Kurt Iron Arse, Imad was neither neurotic nor too young for me.

Had Kurt fetched a second helping of dessert and witnessed the scene between me and the chef or not? I looked around. No Kurt anywhere. Had he perhaps got a bit jealous and left before me?

No, he was standing outside the dining room smoking and he whined, 'There you are at last. While I drop dead from waiting, that mangy moggy is probably tearing our coconut mat to pieces.'

'That bloody mat,' I said, 'doesn't even belong to us. And you're a wimp.'

But Fuzzball was a clever cat or maybe just streetwise. Somehow she knew that I was favourably disposed towards her and that conspiracy was likely to be the most successful tactic; in any case, she wasn't sitting outside our hut.

Kurt immediately got into bed and there he emptied virtually a whole bottle of red wine on his own because, as he put it, he needed to calm down.

When he was fast asleep, and I got up and opened the door again, two phosphorus-green ellipses were glinting at me from a hibiscus hedge. 'Puss, puss,' I said to attract her; and Fuzzball came and brushed against my legs, purring, until I unwrapped the slice of fried fish I'd pinched from the buffet and kept in a paper napkin, and dropped it on the ground. She didn't eat it on the spot, though, but took the piece of fish carefully in her teeth, shook it like a mouse whose neck needed breaking and vanished back into the bushes.

And we repeated this at regular intervals, the cat and I. I slung on my shoulder bag every evening, as a plastic bag might have raised Kurt's suspicions, stole away again from our table during the meal to the fish or meat receptacles, quickly packed up a few tasty morsels and slipped them into my bag. Once we'd got back and Kurt was asleep, I would sneak outside, peel the sodden paper from the food I'd squirrelled away for Fuzzball and call quietly to her. This wasn't necessary, as after a couple of days Fuzzball knew roughly when feeding time was. It was more or less an appointment: the door creaked, I appeared and she came towards me, thin tail aloft, on silent paws and without a single miaow.

I enjoyed going behind Kurt's back like this, striking secret alliances with a cat he hated and a man I liked, the Tunisian chef—probably the least talented but most congenial cook in the whole of North Africa. So, as soon as I'd provided for the cat, I would often return to the dining room along the back of which, facing the sea, were the staff bungalows.

Almost every night I would see Imad sitting on the wooden stairs outside his digs, smoking and drinking a cold beer.

'There you are, Asta la vista,' he said when I stood facing him, and he would get up and wedge the filled ice bucket containing three more beers under one arm and put the other around my waist. We would wander seawards to a jetty a little away from the bathing beach, sit down, gaze out over the water and, usually in silence, empty our bottles, he his second, I both of mine.

Kurt didn't notice a thing, neither that I'd slipped out nor that, about an hour later, I would crawl back into bed with him. And he didn't wake up before ten o'clock in the morning anyway, never—except for once.

The night before that one time, Imad had been waiting for me not with beer but with two bottles of Vignerons de Carthage Magon Majus Gran Vin de Mornag.

'This,' he said, 'is a very big secret and Tunisia's best wine. I have it with me because today we celebrate my birthday.'

The sky above us was full of stars and the wine was very good. I rested my head on Imad's shoulder, and he patted my cheek but didn't kiss me. This I didn't take as an affront, oh no; I saw it as a sign of respect, respect for a foreign woman who'd not come to his country alone and would leave it again once her holiday was over. —I hadn't told him that I knew Djerba and the hospital there well, indeed I had said precious little about myself.

This time we sat together for a long while, longer than usual; Imad's fine wine demanded to be drunk in measured fashion, and there was after all a bottle per head, had Imad been as greedy as me.

As we said goodbye, the sun was already rising out of the sea. I didn't stagger but I must have been pretty drunk and tired and correspondingly careless. I just wanted to sleep.

I only noticed that Fuzzball had managed to dart into our bungalow with me when Kurt reared up, screaming, kicking and sneezing, and then rounded on me: 'When did you let the bloody cat in? What do you think the two of you are doing? Are you trying to kill me?!'

Fuzzball had obviously invaded not only the hut but also our bed at some point, but she hadn't sought out a spot beside me, her snoring benefactor. No, either completely innocently or very mischievously, she had curled up on the quietly breathing Kurt until, just this once, he'd woken up, either due to her purring or my snoring.

Of course, who else but I had to grab the animal and put it outside. But that wasn't the end of the matter. Oh no, there was a ferocious row during which I obviously withheld the fact that I had a pretty good idea how this in Kurt's view 'outrageous incident' had occurred. However, I refused to accept Kurt's insinuation that I'd deliberately lured Fuzzball inside to test and rile him. And so one word led to another and eventually I declared categorically that it was inhuman not to feed a pregnant cat, naturally always at a good distance from the panic-stricken allergy sufferer with whom I was currently forced to endure one of the lousiest periods of my life.

He then threatened me: 'If I come across this or any other cat inside this bungalow again, I will seek someone out and pay them to drown it.'

He shouldn't have said that! Now our domestic bliss was well and truly shattered.

We did still go down to the water and to eat, but separately. I'd never been very talkative, but now I didn't want to talk to Kurt or so much as look at him until, well, until something else happened.

It was our fifth day in Hammamet-Yasmine and, as always so far, we went down to the beach straight after breakfast. Kurt was lying under the parasol; I was sitting reading. However, the roar of the sea was louder than normal that day; an unusually stiff breeze was wafting a disgusting stench of frying food over to us from the nearer snack bars and even the more distant ones. To our left, some event managers from our holiday village were doing lucrative business with the Tunisian brothers-in-law of one of the holiday reps, receptionists or gardeners. For 40 dinar, 10 dollars or 20 deutschmarks per person and per third of an hour, they pulled tourists along over the sea on a colourful, parachute-like contraption. —Nowadays this cure for boredom, correctly known as parasailing, is to be found in every damn tourist spot, but I think it was pretty new at the time.

Kurt could watch this 'spectacle', as he called it, for ever and probably felt like having a go himself, but every time a flyer's particularly shrill shrieking made me look up, I felt kind of queasy.

There was only one of these canopies, and before it got going, the customer—usually a man—was strapped into a harness connected to the canopy by a number of lines. Next to these, on both sides, ran thick straps, the left-hand one wrapped in blue duct tape, the right-hand one in red; the person in the seat had to tug hard on the red one, as they'd been shown, as soon as the small, manoeuvrable motorboat, having pulled them out above the sea and along the coast, returned to the shore.

The organizers had marked out a stretch of sand for take-off and landing where, other than their booth, only the next customer or *pilote*, as they elegantly called him in French, stood. The single brightly coloured parasail canopy was in constant use, the waiting list long, and so far it had all gone smoothly. Eventually, though, there came the moment that changed everything.

I'd be lying if I claimed to have anticipated what was going, yes, what was *bound* to happen, maybe because the Tunisians were dazzled by dollar signs and hadn't factored in humans' innate unpredictability. Did they have no fear or were they simply not imaginative enough to feel any? Did they see tourists only as a small, insignificant cog in a highly profitable mechanism that they'd devised and developed and therefore trusted arrogantly, that is, blindly? —I didn't and don't know.

The look on the face of the fat young German woman who was shoved in front of the parasailing operators' booth around 11 o'clock that day was sceptical or anxious actually, and her reluctance seemed genuine, not pretend. Yet the fat woman could hardly bottle out, as this flight over the sea was a present from her posse, who surrounded her, hooting, in expectation of seeing the 'coward'—that was exactly what one of her nasty friends called her—rise into the air any minute 'like a pumpkin dragon'.

I hoped in vain that the woman would be too large for the peculiar harness or that one of the two Tunisians trying to help her would have some reservations. She barely listened as they explained the role of the cables, especially the red-taped one, in short English sentences, and her face was as white as whey as she clung to the cables to her left and right as if they were the only things offering her any security.

And off went the airmail parcel. The young German floated up and away; all that could be seen were her limp, dangling, sturdy little legs—and then, when she was soaring fairly high in the sky, her head slumped forward on her chest and her hands released the cables.

What had happened? Had she fainted? Or maybe she'd had a heart attack or a stroke? That was what the enterprising Tunisians, though completely unprepared for this scenario, were asking themselves and one another as they followed their canopy open-mouthed and began to gesticulate wildly to their pal in the motorboat to immediately break off the flight, turn round and initiate the landing procedure. But how could this work if the *pilote* didn't play along?

'That woman,' said Kurt, who had leapt to his feet, 'looks like Obelix,' before correcting himself: 'Obelix as a corpse.'

'No,' I countered, 'she's hanging there like blancmange in braces.'

The other bathers were now fully aware that disaster was looming above their heads and were screaming in a cacophony of different languages to give the inert woman instructions or at least to wake her up.

The motorboat altered its course, bringing the parasailing canopy it was towing closer to shore, but the woman hanging from it still didn't come to her senses. So the boot sped back out to sea, perhaps playing for time in the hope that the inexplicable helplessness up there in the sky and the disorganized helplessness down here on the ground would sort itself out.

And so it went on for a while: seawards, beachwards, seawards . . . But nothing changed. The wind obviously made it impossible—or too dangerous—to close the canopy and let it plunge into the water with the woman; if, as we onlookers hoped, the young woman really had only lost consciousness, this manoeuvre would probably have killed her. No one, not even a lifeguard, would have reached her in time. —What about the man driving the motorboat? Count him out, I told myself, there's an age-old tradition of seamen being unable to swim. —The woman therefore had to land, whatever the cost. And that's what she did, and I assume, in the absence of any hard facts to this day, that it did indeed cost her her life.

The boat was heading for land again when there was suddenly a very strong gust of wind from the left which drove the canopy at speed towards a concrete block, a modern high-rise hotel with a wide wooden terrace jutting out far over the sea. There, against the hotel's 50-metre-high, windowless, whitewashed right-hand sidewall, it all ended—an ending no one wanted. The seat harness with the woman in it smashed into this wall, and in its lee the canopy folded in on itself like a collapsed soufflé. And when both, first the woman and then the parasail wing, had reached the bottom, no onlooker who wasn't in the immediate vicinity of the hotel could see either the woman or the canopy any longer, but something new instead: a long blood-red streak running almost vertically from about the centre of the upper third of the wall to a point hidden from them by a forest of parasols.

Frozen like pillars of salt, we bathers and the Tunisians stared at this streak for several seconds or minutes. A profound silence reigned, broken only by the roaring of the sea. —I fancy that I clearly witnessed the unconscious and perhaps already dead, fat, young German woman's skull colliding with the wall. —To this day and right now, since I can't help thinking about it, I reckon I distinctly heard a short, sudden crack, like the sound of a coconut hitting a harder surface.

About a quarter of an hour later, the wailing of an ambulance siren broke the spell. It was perhaps this that allowed us to find our tongues again, some in one tongue, others in another, and, whispering about what we'd witnessed, we packed up our beach equipment. Kurt and I were among those who trotted with bowed heads up the beaten track to their bungalows.

The menacing storm had narrowly skirted Hammamet; and as the two of us entered the dining room, separately of course, and then sat down at the same table and half-heartedly but hungrily polished off a plate of pasta with sauce each, the weather was once more as beautiful as it always is in this part of the world.

After dinner we had the next surprise of the fifth day of our holiday. Or rather, Kurt was surprised, I less so and, unlike Kurt, only in a positive way. Fuzzball had given birth! She was lying next to one of the hibiscus bushes separating our hut from our right-hand neighbours, surrounded by six blind, squeaking baby kittens. The cat, which I could obviously no longer call Fuzzball, gave me a long—and proud, I thought—stare. Her look reminded me of a story my grandma sometimes told me as a child when we were alone together.

When she lived in Meuselwitz near Altenburg, Grandma said, she'd had a cat called Minka. Minka hadn't been neutered—people didn't waste money on such things in the past—and so at least once per year Minka would have kittens.

'And when another of her litters was coming,' Grandma said, 'Minka would mewl and demand that I drop everything and sit down, just as I was, in my house dress; it always had to be the same one, maybe because of the particular smell of this specific robe. I only owned two house dresses at the time anyway, and however regularly I washed those dresses, both of them, Minka would always recognize the one she required to give birth. And if I happened to be wearing the wrong one, I would have to take the correct one out of the dirty washing or off the clothesline and put it on.

'As soon as I sat down on the bench by the stove in Minka's favourite dress, she would jump up onto my lap, elegantly despite her round tum, and have her babies there. It could take hours, depending on how many kittens were waiting to come out, but I wasn't allowed to move or help her; Minka wouldn't even let me touch her.

'Only when the last baby had popped out and the placenta been eaten would she let me stand up and place the tiny things, of which there were usually six and occasionally eight, in a little basket I'd prepared and lined with old but clean bits of cloth.'

'And what about the kittens? You didn't keep them all?' I asked.

'Well,' Grandma replied, 'that wasn't so easy. So Minka didn't go mad I would always let her nurse her brats until they lost interest in her milk, then offered the nicest ones from each litter to people nearby. The ones I couldn't get rid of were dropped into a sack and drowned in Meuselwitz's fire pond by a neighbour's son who had no objections and possibly even fun doing it, because Emil certainly wasn't the squeamish type.'

I shed a few tears over this, this being so many cute little pussycats meeting such a gruesome end. And Grandma gave me half a glass of her homemade egg liqueur and wept along with me, though probably not for Minka and her kittens.

And one time, just the once, Grandma appended another story to this one.

'Your mother Anneliese,' said Grandma, 'was always completely daft about Minka's babies when she was little. And so it happened, one evening when I wasn't paying attention and didn't say goodnight to her because she'd been naughty, that Anneliese took three of the kittens to bed and cuddled them until she fell asleep. The next morning the little cats were dead, all three of them; Anneliese must have had nightmares and tossed and turned in her sleep, squashing them. After that your mother only cared for dogs. She had no time for cats any more.'

I knew how clever my black-and-white-striped Tunisian cat was and so I'd have loved to tell her Grandma's story, but I couldn't, and still can't, speak either Arabic or French and consider animals, even highly developed ones, incapable of even beginning to understand human language, no matter which.

Of course I talked to her just the same. —I did occasionally talk, when I still talked, to far more stupid creatures or even things, especially when they didn't work the way I wanted them to. —'Well done, pussycat, very well done,' I said. And the fledgling mother cat purred and let me stroke her, though she did hold her paws and her thin tail protectively over her babies.

Following that terrible fifth day, relations between Kurt and me improved somewhat, probably down to our *shared* experience and the shock that affected us and most other witnesses for some time afterwards.

The morning after the accident, however, the parasailing hut had vanished without a trace, as if the event had never happened.

Otherwise, we settled back into our normal routine: we swam, lay in the sun and ate badly. At night I fed the cat, which naturally needed more and better food now.

Imad, whom I continued to meet in secret, slipped me raw meat and the odd fresh fish as I'd asked him to, although if he'd known about it, he would probably have found it hard to understand my hobby. But he didn't ask and simply fulfilled my requests. And the cat, which had made itself at home with her young under her favourite hibiscus bush and only let me serve her there, grew stronger, her coat shinier and her babies bigger.

Even if we, Kurt and I, argued less now, we nevertheless welcomed every day that passed and brought us closer to our departure. Without having discussed it, we knew it was over. We would split up. Kurt was probably also asking himself whether we'd ever really been together. We were incompatible; this Tunisian holiday had made that abundantly clear.

Curiously, though, it was precisely this enforced yet time-limited proximity, which we could not yet entirely avoid, that made the last three weeks relatively bearable. During the day, Kurt went his way— and I went mine as soon as night fell. Kurt no longer moaned about the cat or gave a fig about its babies, which grew rapidly, becoming ever prettier and livelier. He would often buy himself two or three bottles of wine or have cocktails with the holiday reps by the pool; he went to the harbour and took photos of the boats and the sea. I read, fed the big cat, played with the little ones, met Imad and slept for even longer than Kurt.

However, one morning, two days before we left, I woke up very early because the cat was miaowing loudly outside, closer than for a long time, and the six kittens were squeaking at a very high pitch. I was afraid something had happened, so I got up and went to have a look.

My pussycat had dragged her babies onto the doormat. And if one of the kittens tried to leave the mat and wriggle off somewhere, she would grab it by the scruff of its neck and put it back in its place.

'What are you doing?' I said. 'Didn't you have enough to eat last night? Wait a second, I'll fetch you a tasty little morsel.'

The cat stared me in the eye, stonily and beseechingly, yet also somehow unwaveringly, as if she were trying to hypnotize me—and then shot off like greased lightning with one final screech, louder than any she'd ever made before. Was it a cry for help? An order? Something along the lines of 'Over to you, Asta Arnold! I've done my bit. I want my freedom. Now it's your turn to look after them, because you and you alone hold the key to what my offspring need now'?

I scampered around between the bungalows, calling the cat by a name that no longer applied to it. 'Fuzzball, Fuzzball,' I called, and someone shouted back, 'When the hell are we finally going to get some peace and quiet around here?'

About an hour later I was standing outside our bungalow again, sadly without having accomplished anything. I'd come across a number of cats—God knows there were enough of them around—but not mine. I couldn't see three of the kittens my cat had deposited and abandoned on the mat, not at first anyway; they had set up on their own—or set out to look for their mother—, heading off in different directions, though none of them had covered more than a couple of metres. The three other, less hardy ones were still sitting on the doormat, whining and squeaking dolefully, kneading the mat with their paws and snagging their tiny claws in the woven coir fibres, which looked funnier than it was.

I opened our bungalow door, shot Kurt, who was no longer asleep and scowling reproachfully at me, a glare that made him want to dive back under the covers, searched for a cardboard box and when, as expected, I couldn't find one, opted for my suitcase. You won't need it, I told myself bitterly, until the day after tomorrow.

I fetched the kittens, put them in the suitcase and zipped it up, though not all the way obviously—the young ones had to be able to breathe but not run away.

All that Kurt could think to say as he watched me from the bed was, 'That suitcase has to go outside.'

Without answering I carried the suitcase outside, even though Kurt had just fled the bed and the entire scene in nothing but his swimming trunks.

It's for the best, I thought and went my own way too. How do you feed three-week-old baby cats, I wondered. Can they digest anything other than their mother's milk yet?

I walked into the dining room, but not for breakfast; no, I quickly grabbed a handful of soft bread and a few pre-cut slices of liver sausage and poured warm cow's milk into an empty coke bottle I'd found between two bungalows.

It went down a treat. The kittens fell upon the bread I'd soaked in milk and mixed with snippets of sausage as if there were no tomorrow. And that was how it was, pretty much. That's because, I thought, I can take care of you tomorrow but not the day after.

The youngsters had made quite a mess, spattering the lining of my suitcase and peeing and pooing. I'd hurriedly wiped away everything that could be wiped away with a towel, which of course didn't belong to me. Then, finally, it went quiet inside the suitcase! The dear little things were purring, sated and peaceful and snuggled into a cute bundle. This pretty sight didn't really comfort me, though, or not for long. I had to be off again.

I did all I could, searching high and low for the black-and-white-striped cat all over the property and even enquiring about her to every person I met; most of them gave at best a regretful shrug, others had seen a cat but not mine. Mine, I gradually realized, had vanished without a trace—and she didn't return, not to her kittens, not to me, not that afternoon, not that evening, not that night nor the next day.

Had I interpreted that look correctly? Had she left her litter to me, unaware that I would soon be leaving Hammamet? Or had something happened to her? But if that were the case and my pussycat were dead, I told myself, then wouldn't I have at least stumbled upon her mortal remains? Maybe, I mused, she'd been chased, wounded and devoured by a larger predator, all hide and hair of her, or rather from her whiskers to her tail. But would that kind of animal, a wolf, a lynx or a wild dog venture into a crowded tourist resort like this?

As I continued to imagine the blackest scenario, a horrible thought crossed my mind. 'Kurt,' I cried angrily, 'could you do such a thing? Might you have throttled my cat with your bare hands and buried her somewhere or chucked her into the sea?!'

Kurt planted himself in front of me, legs wide apart, hands on his chubby hips. 'You should know by now,' he said icily, as always on this particular subject, 'that I wouldn't touch that creature, not even with a pair of pliers. See any pliers here? And if I did have a pair of pliers or tongs handy, don't you think I'd have done away with her six little sprogs at the same time?!'

I can't remember the last day of the holiday, only the last night; it was bad—maybe not the worst of my life, but bad enough.

Oddly it was raining, so hard that I didn't feel like sitting outside our hut—nor did I feel like lying next to Kurt, whose backside was soft and pink, not iron really, but, was poking out from under the covers. I dragged my pillow from the bed and hunkered down in a corner. Clutching my pillow to my stomach, I wept quietly for a while. But since I couldn't—or didn't want to—sleep and had to come up with a solution or at least a temporary solution, at some point I struggled to my feet and bundled the kittens into a sweater, one I knew I'd miss less than them. I carried Fuzzball's offspring to the staff quarters but not to Imad's bungalow. He wasn't waiting for me with beer as usual that night because we'd already said our good-byes, briefly and tersely due to my gloomy mood.

As day broke, I returned to the slumbering Kurt, cleaned my suitcase as best I could and packed.

Afterwards, as it was no longer raining, I sat down beside the orphaned hibiscus bushes for a smoke. I didn't go to breakfast, nor did I check on the cats again. I was far too scared that they might squeal miserably or might even have vanished—like their mother. Among all these holiday guests or the kitchen and cleaning staff, I sought to convince myself, there must be one sympathetic soul who'd take care of those little ones. If not, then . . . I refused to imagine what then.

On the bus to Tunis airport Kurt sat up front behind the driver and I sat beside an ageing, peroxide-blonde Dutch woman who was flicking through a somewhat dated fashion magazine and, without offering me one, gorging herself on biscuits.

There was no changing the fact that we still had to sit next to each other on the plane because the tickets had already been issued and were part of our travel documents. I didn't even deign to look at Kurt, staring instead at the book lying open in front of me but incapable of reading. Kurt took no notice of me either. He acted as if he didn't know me; no, as if I were the neighbour he'd never have opted for had he been given the choice.

Did we break up at Vienna Schwechat airport? Not even, I don't think. We dragged our respective suitcases off the luggage belt and walked away, one this way, the other that. Kurt didn't look round, and nor did I.

As I went down to the platforms to wait for the next shuttle train, I considered where in Vienna I might get a hotel room for the three nights before I departed for Bonn and the headquarters of CARE Germany, and whether I'd left any belongings, anything important, at Kurt's, but I could think of nothing.

That was it for Kurt and me. We never saw each other again; no final letter, no phone call, no nothing.

A sta gets up awkwardly from the neglected patch of lawn where the long-gone cat had been sitting. Her backside is damp even though the thunderstorm finished some time ago, but her mouth is so dry she doesn't even fancy lighting another cigarette. I should, she thinks, go through that revolving door and have a drink inside, not necessarily a disgustingly sweet Diet Coke costing four euros that would probably taste even shittier here than elsewhere because I've noticed it still isn't common in Germany to dilute soft drinks with ice. And besides, I'd have to pay for my beverage by credit card. The alternative would be a gulp of tap water, which I could get in the restrooms free. Some coins or notes wouldn't hurt, though. *Notes*, another peculiar word, as if all it required were a few lines or a little tune to get a cocktail. —I could do with one right now. So why not finally go and look for a cash machine? Because then I couldn't avoid speaking a few words of English or German, not to the cash machine but to one of the women or men at this counter here or elsewhere.

You're not allowed to speak, only think. Think and keep your mouth shut! Who, Asta wonders, is ordering me around. My inner voice? Is that even my voice? It sounds like mine, but *is* it mine? Sometimes I'm pretty sure it is, others I'm not.

A man comes shooting out of the revolving door beside which Asta is loitering. He nearly, Asta thinks with amusement, got his timing wrong and went for another spin on the carousel. The man looks annoyed. No, Asta thinks, more like insulted or humiliated.

He's short and slim, his age hard to guess, maybe only 65, maybe over 70. Wedged between his flawless, snow-white teeth, which look real or in any case not like generic dentures, is a fat cigar, probably a Havana. He's wearing a black suit and under the jacket a yellow shirt with a tie, whose knot he—or someone else?—has not only loosened but undone so that the ends of the somewhat creased red-and-blue-chequered strip of material are dangling over his left and right lapels. Like a noose he knows is too short for him to hang himself with, thinks Asta. —Isn't he that actor from back then in New York, or possibly even the man that actor played? I've forgotten the names of the film, the actor and the character, like so many others in recent times. Obviously that dishevelled old bloke, who's getting a little stroppy because his cigar keeps going out and who's gazing past me as if hasn't picked up on my shameless staring, could just as well be his brother or doppelgänger. But whose brother or doppelgänger? The actor's or the Nazi doctor's he played so convincingly that for days afterwards I wondered whether he wasn't afraid of being mistaken for the original doctor and spat at by passers-by in the street who'd been to the cinema before, with or after me, or even by an elderly person who'd miraculously escaped from a concentration camp—why not the man that didn't feature in the film and yet was its real subject.

But maybe the actor, that is, the man fiddling about over there by the revolving door, trying to ignore me, doesn't look much like the man he played. Hardly anyone knows what the actual would-be murderer really looked like back then and whether he's still alive and has possibly undergone cosmetic surgery. Nazi bigwigs, in any case those who slipped through the net of the victors' justice, have often lived to a ripe old age; and surely many of them had stashed away some cash when it became clear that the Third Reich was coming to an end, enough to take steps to conceal their identity, or else enjoyed the support of secret, filthy-rich benefactors who not only put them up for years but also afford an Argentinian, Brazilian or Paraguayan plastic surgeon. So it isn't entirely impossible that the man over there, now finally lowering his gaze and stepping slightly to one side, is indeed *the* man, the despicable fascist the film was about.

The film, although I suddenly feel as if it might all have been a dream, was—or is, if it really did and does exist—a feature film, but it was shot like a documentary, with all the typical stylistic attributes of a late '40s or early '50s documentary. It was shot in black and white and in English; none of the actors seemed to be professional, and the cases it tackled were absolutely authentic. 'Cases', yes, because throughout the film's entire one-and-a-half-hour running time all we viewers saw was the courtroom, not a single image, not even a photograph of, or from, the little-known concentration camp it was about. And it wasn't actually about the camp in the former Territory of the Chief of Civil Administration of Alsace, but about five doctors who had indulged in sadistic atrocities under the guise of research and now sat hunched beside their respective defence lawyers for long passages of the film.

I still know who invited me to the cinema, though. It was Andy, Andreas Rudolph; but in New York, where he bred lab animals for a university hospital, he called himself Andy.

Nurse Sylvia, with whom I'd shared a room for the first few weeks of my five years at HAN, had given me the address of her brother Andreas and a parcel, a present I was supposed to deliver to him, before I flew to New York to attend another UNICEF-funded training course. Quite rightly none of us trusted the Nicaraguan postal service, and so she seized the opportunity to use me as a courier.

Andy was delighted with Sylvia's gift—it was an antiquarian English-language edition of Jean-Baptiste de Lamarck's *Zoological Philosophy*—and also no doubt by the variety a visit from one of his sister's friends brought to his fairly lonely life. He took me out to dinner, showed me Chinatown, Central Park and the Bronx and, on one occasion, all the laboratory rats and mice he took such loving care of and whose fate touched him more than he liked to admit.

One night, we were standing in the permanent orange glow from the low basement ceiling of his 'kingdom', as he called it. Andy reached into one of the cages, and three tiny, naked, blind baby mice immediately curled themselves around his wide male palm like worms.

'Look,' he said, 'look at their tummies. These babies' skin is still paper-thin and transparent. You can see immediately that their bellies are brimming, brimming with rich white mother's milk. And now look, now they're peeing and shitting, not out of fear, though, but because they feel almost as safe with me as with their mum in the sawdust.'

The cinema we went to two days later was named—or is named, should it still exist—after a woman; I can remember that, oddly enough, although the woman's actual name has slipped my mind. The cinema was in downtown New York, on Houston Street in Greenwich Village; its slightly kitsch theatre décor and highbrow programme, Andy reckoned, made it very popular with students and lecturers from nearby NYU, and he too found it so cosy that he used to spend many a Sunday there.

There was a delicious aroma of roasted corn in the foyer, and I'd already fished out my purse when Andy said, 'We'd be better off without popcorn and beer today because what we're about to see is tough stuff.'

'You mean you know this film?' I asked.

But Andy merely gave me a flinty look and made a roof with both forefingers against his lips—a sign he often made when he didn't wish to speak or wanted to halt the other person's stream of words.

No, I cannot merely have dreamt that film, and Andy even less so—I'm not that imaginative or mad—but it might not have been anything like I remember it. I'd have to ask Andy since he was there. —Knowing me, though, I won't ask him. I'm not going to try to find out Andy's address again or refresh and rekindle something. That chance has passed.

The film—perhaps it's still out there but no one shows it any more—didn't begin chronologically like the famous documentary about the Nuremberg doctors' trial which had obviously inspired the director, nor did it begin with the four doctors, whose criminal experiments on humans were at the core of this trial or, to be precise, of this main hearing, being escorted into the courtroom by men in uniform, but with the final statement that each of the accused was allowed to make before he heard his sentence.

Was the hearing held before a US military tribunal or in a French court? I can't remember, only that one of the four bastards who had *followed their bizarre orders* in this concentration camp—the fifth was dead and could therefore no longer be called to account—

incriminated himself, albeit not regarding his deeds or misdeeds. No, unlike the other three, who, as expected, refused to acknowledge any guilt for the charges, and when the judge invited them to have their final say, merely dragged up the familiar patriotic clichés of loyalty to the Führer and the Fatherland, one of them—the same one who's currently pacing about very close to me around this ugly chrome ashtray full of wet butts, puffing on a cigar—insisted that he had genuinely wanted everything to happen as it did and had been willing to 'eliminate worthless life'.

'Yes,' cried this small fidgety man with thick, astonishingly black hair, comical round metal-rimmed spectacles, a scar next to his sensual mouth and the canny expression of an actor, 'I am guilty, guilty of betraying the National Socialist ideal and my colleagues and brothers-in-arms whom I bitterly let down through my weakness, a weakness for which I still cannot supply a reason or an explanation!'

And as his coxcomb continued to grow and he continued to crow in his shrill, harshly accented voice, as if he were authentically German, a German who spoke passable English, and his face swelled up more and more and tears came to his eyes, tears of shame, not of remorse; they rolled unchecked down his pale, clean-shaven cheeks, and his voice began to quaver with the strength of his emotion.

And then, from off-screen or from the heavens, as it were, a narrator, who of course never revealed himself in physical form, drowned out this madman. This particular defendant, a gynaecologist from Lower Lusatia, the viewers were now told, had only become active at the camp in Alsace later, sometime in the autumn of 1943 and at his own request. —More like inactive, I thought, because he had after all not been capable of acting according to Hitler's or the others' will. —To assimilate quickly into the conspiratorial five-strong group of doctors, the voice said approximately, his colleagues had made him undergo an initiation rite they regarded as a prerequisite for his integration. And so on the day this little man—whom I shall call Dr A.—arrived, he was presented with a woman, a French Jew or a resistance fighter, he didn't know for sure; a pretty, untouched young woman.

Here there was a cut; the cinemagoers were transported back to an earlier stage of the hearing when the lawyers and their clients had been permitted to describe events from their own perspective. And once again we heard Dr A. whose curious failure had provided the opportunity for the actor portraying him to take on the major role, perhaps the greatest and most terrible role of his entire and otherwise not exactly successful artistic career.

'To this woman, who was neither asleep nor anaesthetized, merely strapped down,' he said, quietly now, 'I was to administer an injection of 20 millilitres of petrol directly into the heart muscle, and I was determined to do it because I wanted to become a fully fledged member of our community as quickly as possible. But the operation must have been too difficult for me, might have been too much even for a real tough guy . . . Please, comrades,' Dr A. stammered, looking round at them, 'please do not misconstrue what I'm saying. I'm not trying to justify myself. I would've liked to be like you; that's what I longed for in my heart of hearts. And to this very day I feel close to you and regret only that ridiculous, innate flaw that prevented me from emulating you. Believe me, I too considered our inmates, one and all, to be enemies and subhumans, and I had not the slightest scruple regarding the task at which, more than once, I failed so pathetically. But, as you know, that woman looked at me with her big, dark eyes and I quite literally fell to the ground, simply fell to the ground.'

And once more he turned to the other three and looked as if he were struggling not to cry before eventually letting the tears flow.

'Understandably,' he continued through his sobs, 'you all teased me and you, Major, called me "sissy" and the "limpest gherkin in the jar". But I was involved now and knew what we were up to, so you gave me a second chance and even a third . . . '

Then there was another cut, and Dr A. became smaller and quieter and eventually fell silent for a while; all we could see were his lips moving. The narrator took over; the four others, all practised doctors, the voice said, had done all they could to help the newcomer. —Unfortunately, I thought, only three of the four are now sitting in the dock, three in addition to Dr A., who is actually standing, three whose clenched fists suggest they would dearly love to leap to their feet and do what, if they hadn't been so cowardly, they ought to have done long ago, namely to silence this blabbermouth for good.

'The others felt that the next time,' the voiceover continued, 'the newcomer absolutely must pass the test. They therefore had a frail, shaven-headed older woman brought before him, one of the people they had injected with murine typhus and treated with drugs as part of the second control group.'

Nevertheless, like the young, healthy woman before her, this woman too—and the gang of four doctors refused to compromise on this—was not anaesthetized. One look and again Dr A. crumpled to the floor.

For the third and final attempt, the bastards would have said to themselves, OK, our oversensitive rookie is a gynaecologist by training, so female prisoners, young or old, are problematic. If it had been possible to get rid of Dr A., they would have forced him to keep his mouth shut and given him a sideways promotion—or done away with him like any old prisoner and made up some fail-safe story about an accident. Unfortunately, however, as we viewers now learnt, Dr A. was the deputy camp commander's nephew, and this inconvenient fact compelled them to pursue a more humane alternative; and so the gang of four decided to set the bar so low that he could hop over it.

A man was pushed into the operating theatre for Dr A., a skeletal bald old man with hollow, stubbly cheeks, an individual who looked as if a sudden end would be preferable to the excruciating death that awaited him in any case two or three days hence. Yet this old man was also conscious and stared at him with big, dark eyes. And Dr A.'s wits deserted him; once more he swooned and lay unconscious for at least five minutes on the theatre tiles.

The gang would and could do no more or no less for this 'damp squib', as Dr A. referred to himself during his final statement. 'No,' he quoted, almost admiringly, the former SS Sturmbannführer and the major sitting three chairs away from him in his following sentence, 'can't we give this little wimp a dead man to kill so he can finally stay upright?!'

In the one and a half years that remained before the Allies' victory, the gang of four bullied their fellow Nazi Dr A. very subtly and with the consent of a man who was clearly racked with self-loathing even then. Since there was little demand for his true specialization, gynaecology, as only two higher-ranking comrades had moved into villas near the camp with their spouses and children, and the rest of the staff included no more than five women, he had to perform a series of additional and auxiliary tasks, anything that came up and wasn't entirely beneath the dignity of a relative of the deputy camp commander, a Nazi Party member and a doctor: labelling tissue samples, recording trial data, writing death certificates, keeping lists of materials, filing correspondence and occasionally, if it happened to suit one of the gang's research needs, assisting with pathology.

Were there closing arguments? There must have been, but I can't remember them, probably because the rapid English spoken by those playing the prosecutor and the defence lawyers had gradually worn me out; I can only recall the verdicts and the opinion of the court being announced, but this section of the film passed fairly quickly, a lot more quickly than in a real trial.

Then there was another cut. For about quarter of an hour we saw alternating scenes of the chief justice reading out the sentences and the hunched figures of the defendants; and in both rooms, the court-room and the cinema, *deathly silence* reigned.

And, indeed, what we had all hoped for came to pass. Three of the four doctors were sentenced to death, although I can't remember whether it was by hanging or guillotine. One of them collapsed when he heard his name with the guilty verdict. He had to be caught as he fell and propped up by two uniformed guards who had rushed to his aid because his defence lawyers, though standing to the left and right of him, didn't lift a finger; on the contrary, they sneered at their client's fainting fit.

The two other defendants kept their composure when they found out that they were to be executed, looking as if they had been turned to stone and taking their seats only when one of the judges ordered them to do so.

Dr A. was the only one who stared the man wearing the robes of the chief justice in the eye, his head held high, stubbornly, even defiantly. Yet to his astonishment and that of the public, through whose ranks there ran a murmur accompanied by various cries of 'Oh no', he did not receive 20 or, at the least, 10 years in prison, but an out-and-out acquittal.

Dr A. screamed in protest—as did we viewers. 'Why?' he roared. 'Why are you insulting me, Your Honour?!' I demand justice, not mercy! I'm guilty! I want to share the fate of my fellow culprits. Yes, *Kameraden*, I wish to die, die like you . . .'

He was dragged out of the room by several guards, presumably because the high court would no longer stand for his provocative out-cry, but even this he resisted fiercely.

The penultimate scene of the film showed Dr A. a few weeks later on a bench in an autumnal park. He was sitting there like a coachman on a box seat, his slender hands resting between his sharp knees, visible through his woollen trousers. The wind ruffled his shock of hair, which no longer seemed quite so thick and dark at the temples. Yet his film-star face still looked smooth and soft and somehow even handsome due to the melancholy, broken expression he had dis-played during the hearing too, even when he was angry.

'Obviously,' Dr A. said to the camera, 'I am very, very sad. I think constantly of my brothers-in-arms. I write to each of them every day. None of them has ever replied, but I can understand that. I will do my best to comfort their widows and children at least. Luckily, I have no family of my own other than an uncle who has been languishing in jail for a long time and will probably die there. And the sword of death hanging over the heads of my brothers-in-arms might come down at any moment. Then I will no longer even have this elective affinity. Then I'll be completely alone in a defeated and devastated country that used to be my homeland . . .'

At the word 'homeland', or actually after the words 'elective affinity', by which this pitiful phrasemonger merely sought to show that he knew his Goethe, I switched off inside. But other viewers were murmuring again—or still—and some started to laugh because Dr A. just would not stop. No, he blathered on and on, bombastically and yet so urgently that I too began to find him comical, even felt a tiny bit sorry for him—and was tempted to forget who was actually blathering; an actor, a really good actor, I had to admit, namely the guy over there who has now tossed the remains of his cigar next to, rather than into, the ashtray and is heading back to the revolving door to blend into the scurry of people beyond the glass wall before I could potentially confront him, if, well, if I could . . .

The film ended similarly to my present experience. Dr A. disappeared. As he blathered on incessantly, the camera pulled away from him, and he became smaller and smaller and quieter and quieter and soon he was no more than a whispering and then silent dot in an enormous park bursting with autumn colour, which also became smaller and smaller and was soon a slightly hilly, red-yellow-and-green patch, as if the cameraman were travelling in a helicopter at the end and had risen up and up into the white of the clouds above countryside that was probably not German but French or American; of that, though I do in fact remember a great deal, I still cannot be sure.

Still mumbling, already quietly arguing among themselves, the viewers rose from the comfortable red velvet cinema seats before the closing credits began to roll. We, Andy and I, also made our way briskly outside. Andy said nothing, but I had to vent my feelings: 'That really was the biggest crock of shit! That arsehole is a fascist, just a weak one incapable of doing what his unwavering convictions required him to do. How could they let him go . . .'

Andy took my arm and guided me to a nearby pub where smoking was still permitted then. Only once we had sat down and Andy had ordered two pints of Samuel Adams and a double-whisky chaser for himself did he say something: 'Why are you so worked up? Whatever that cockroach wanted or didn't want to do is of no importance. He didn't do it, end of story! Either you didn't properly understand the opinion of the court or you weren't listening. It decided that he "backed away from the planned deed and is therefore not liable to prosecution". But did he back away from the deed voluntarily or involuntarily? I'm no legal expert, but I do know that, at least according to the criminal code of the Federal Republic of Germany, that's a pretty important factor and yet, strangely, it wasn't mentioned. Was that the scriptwriter's mistake, or the director's?'

'Voluntarily or involuntarily: that's the key question for me,' I said, 'not whether it was the scriptwriter's or the director's mistake. That imbecile fainted every time he was supposed to murder someone. Or can you faint voluntarily?'

'Who can assess that beyond any possible doubt? A judge? A psychologist?' Andy shot back. 'Maybe the guy was hysterical—it'd be just like him. Or he simply feigned the blackouts, thinking, as long as the others believe I really swooned, then the worst they'll think is that I'm a bottler but not some dangerous do-gooder, an old-school humanist physician who hadn't a clue what was going on here when he arrived. Now he knows, though, he might start writing sentimental letters to some organization or other outside the camp, describing everything in minute detail. And isn't it possible that he had greater reason to fear his murderous mates, even in that courtroom, than eye contact with his potential victims, which is why he kept up his performance and continued his act in the dock and on that park bench!? Maybe he fooled everyone—his loathsome colleagues, the judges, us cinemagoers . . .'

'I don't believe he was that clever!' I objected. 'If that were the case, then the professional actor would've been playing an amateur actor with more talent than he has or had. And that would be *l'art pour l'art*—or, to put it more prosaically, aspic in jelly. No, no, the real Nazi wanted to, but couldn't. He was—and still is, if he's alive—exactly like the rest of that gang: a brainwashed racist but, unfortunately, a squeamish one, no, weak . . . '

'Weak?' Andy cut me off. 'So why did he become a doctor if he couldn't kill anyone? Vets and zookeepers can. They have to be able to.'

To my amazement Andy's face suddenly lit up; he ordered his fourth Jim Beam and one for me too, and said, 'That's beside the point, completely beside the point. Let's assume the story is true and this guy really was the way he presented himself in the film. Would it matter *why* he keeled over every time the person he seriously intended to kill looked at him—"with big, dark eyes", to use his own words. The crucial thing is that he could be *relied upon* to faint. It's conceivable that the three pairs of eyes that sought out his could have been small and bright. And maybe it wasn't the eyes that kept him from killing but the thought: I'm supposed to kill now, kill a human being. Anyway, our actor's role model has probably sobbed himself into the grave by now, but maybe his intriguing flaw wasn't a one-off. Maybe the guy in the film who's got me racking my brains like this belonged to a strange breed of freaks, and maybe that breed hasn't completely died out. What stops us imagining that at this very moment, in my moment of inspiration, there is one, at least one mortal like him who, as if at the flick of a switch, loses consciousness as soon as he's told to kill someone and, for all I know, wants to kill that person? And what distinguishes this particular individual from the many who butcher their fellow men—all of them, victims and butchers, the pride of creation—in cold blood or more reluctantly, but who nonetheless do so when ordered to. And of the seven billion people currently on this earth, maybe not just one but three, four or five would react exactly the same when push came to shove. We need to find and analyse them. And when all the data has been evaluated and the key to this "pacifist blackout", as I shall call it, has been identified, it might perhaps be possible to manipulate or, even better, condition us all, every person on the entire planet that is, male and female, so that if they ever attempted to kill their own kind, they would literally and *instantly* drop unconscious. Let us look into which gene causes unconsciousness or which other aspects of Homo *sapiens* need to be biologically engineered to achieve this effect, and murder and slaughter and war would soon be a thing of the past. And we, together, Asta, would win the Nobel Peace Prize and the one for medicine and heaven knows what other awards. Am I a genius or what?' Andy concluded with a broad grin.

He looked as if he longed to surf the waves of this crazy chain of thought for ever; but in the full fervour of his monologue, he'd been gripped by violent hiccups and they now hurled him back onto the beach of reality.

'A genius?' I said scornfully. 'Why do men always want to be geniuses? I'd rather help and preferably, when it comes to the crunch, not lose consciousness.'

Oh yeah, dear old Andy cooked up a pretty paella of craziness that evening, but so did I.

'What would happen,' I said, 'if just because the needy, for example the seriously wounded, sometimes still die in their helping hands, the thought that it might happen made helpers faint? Aren't the chances of helpers making a difference faint enough already?'

We chatted for a little longer about so-called 'poisonous pedagogy', which advised mothers whose babies were of course still symbiotically attached to them, meaning they didn't have an ego of their own, to breastfeed them at precise intervals, but outside of those fixed times leave them to cry until exhaustion made them fall silent and give up, give up the ghost they'd practically become.

'Babies,' I said, 'die if they aren't fed every few hours somehow by someone. They dehydrate; those little birdies don't know that, but they feel it.'

'So why leave them to cry?' Andy asked.

'They're supposed to learn that humans don't always immediately get their own way,' I said. 'And their mothers are supposed to kindly plug their ears and suppress their instincts.'

'Exactly,' Andy agreed, ordering two more Jim Beams. 'And that,' he continued, slurring his words, 'is how fear develops, this fucking mortal fear that will later enable you to snuff someone out before he snuffs you out.'

'Yeah,' I said, 'that may be true, but it's more true of boys than girls. And almost certainly,' I said with increasing excitement, 'the mother of the Nazi we're talking about would rather have had a girl, which is why she treated and raised her son like one. Seen from that perspective, there's no need for genetic manipulation or recon-ditioning. Maybe everybody, even males, should just be brought up like girls.'

'That's conceivable,' Andy replied, 'but I don't want to be a girl. Besides, there are women murderers too—well, there are nowadays anyway.'

'Not many,' I countered.

'Because they don't usually have to go into the army,' Andy slurred, trying to drown his hiccups in his sixth or tenth Samuel Adams. And I nodded and said no more, as my brain too was becoming foggy with drink.

We got seriously wasted, and at some stage we staggered out into the night and were wholly at one with each other, but still we didn't ask: your place or mine. Maybe because neither of us was capable of even such a simple question—let alone what ought to have followed.

Three days later I flew back to Managua. Two further postcards arrived from Andy, but he might well have sent others that never arrived. I wrote him a letter too; I even, I think, wrote first. But did he receive my letter? There was nothing in the brief messages on the back of his New York postcards to suggest that he had. And then due to my work at HAN I forgot Andy—until today, no, until just now.

O h Andy, you were all right and so bright. Why didn't we form a rodent-breeder-and-nurse couple together? Sounds sweet, doesn't it? Asta thinks. She almost puts her lips together to whistle the tune of the Tom Waits song Andy sometimes sang her, having often listened to the original version since on a record called 'Rain Dogs', Andy's parting gift: 'And it's time, time, time, and it's time, time, time / and it's time, time, time, that you love / and it's time, time, time . . . '

But of course she doesn't and simply shakes a new cigarette from the near-empty first of her ten Camel soft packs, lights up and approaches the revolving door. She presses her forehead to the glass facade beside it; and again her eyes fish in the crowds of people beyond for another vaguely familiar face, but she can't find one—until a woman takes a seat outside the Chinese snack bar, a young woman who puts down her cardboard plate of noodles not on one of the bistro tables but on her lap. In spite of the heat she's wearing an expensive-looking, probably pure silk, cream-coloured headscarf, but not the way Kurdish women would usually wear theirs; no, although hers doesn't cover her fringe, it's pulled tight all the way around and tied behind her neck. That was fashionable in the 1930s, Asta thinks. It was how sporty women protected their little ears from the wind as they rode in red cabriolets beside gentlemen in flat caps and checked jackets.

The woman inside has delicate red lips, a pleasantly propor-
tioned, straight nose, strong brows and, as Asta herself can make out
even from this distance, long black lashes beneath which extremely
unusual eyes twinkle as the woman looks up. Oh, *strabismus divergens*,
Asta thinks. Stella, our one-and-only Nurse Stella, had an even more
beautiful squint, though. And Stella was altogether more beautiful
than this woman.

Stella, the half-Italian from Baden, was tranquillity itself; her
movements flowed gently, serenely even, and yet there was nothing
sluggish, let alone lascivious about them. Stella was more like an
apparition. And yet she wasn't aware of her consummate, well, almost
consummate elegance. And everyone, absolutely everybody, whether
patient, fellow nurse, doctor or other, became completely calm when
Stella's quicksilver squint alighted on him. —Silver?! The effect Stella
had was more like *solid gold*. —Her eyes were large and almond-
shaped—and the colour of amber, like a lion's. When she looked at
someone, and occasionally that someone was me, she didn't look me
in the eye: she couldn't. No, my eyes sought out hers, which took
some doing because Stella's eyes were not a pair but in almost constant and independent motion; I always had the feeling that I needed
to catch one of the two and hold onto it. But Stella's eyes, now this
one, now that, immediately broke free again and rolled around all
over the place, as if the woman to whom they belonged were anxious
not to overlook anything in the vicinity.

Stella wasn't angry at the bilateral exophoria she'd probably had
since birth; she was angry at nothing and nobody. Stella was friendly
to the core, cheerful even, although she never laughed, merely had a

smile so permanent and so faint, no, so ethereal that one wondered, was it a smile at all or just an impression created by the dimples that appeared at the corners of her mouth as soon as her full, soft lips rose ever so slightly.

One of our patients there in the Second Ulan-Bator Clinic, a 12-year-old girl with a heart disorder who'd learnt pretty good German from a father trained as a spinning mill technician in East Germany, once called Stella *the squinting angel*. This was such a fitting nickname that we adopted it, especially since Stella didn't appear to object to it. The squinting angel or Stella or 'starry eyes', as the big-headed head nurse who was incredibly smug about her 'perfect Italian' sometimes called her, didn't mind whether we called her this, that or the other; she would come running and do what she had to do, serenely, skilfully and with that twisted, ungraspably beautiful gaze that no one could ever hold.

Of course, the Mongolian girl had no idea that the nickname she'd given Nurse Stella was doubly appropriate. For Stella, who liked to wear a headscarf, 'out of habit' as she said, had originally wanted to become a nun. Not because her faith was so strong, she said; she'd merely yearned for a structured, fulfilling life, free of the vagaries of an individual fate: life in a convent.

'I'd just completed my medical training at St Joseph's Hospital in Heidelberg and was only 21, but I was already a novice of the Company of the Daughters of Charity of Saint Vincent de Paul,' she told me and four other German CARE International exchange nurses at a Christmas party, her first and last with us, when we asked her how she'd come to be out here in the steppes.

'From early December 1998,' Stella continued, '12 other Vincentians and I had cared around the clock for about 50 sisters of the Company who had worked all their lives in nurseries, boarding schools, homes or hospices and, having reached a ripe old age, now needed caring for themselves.

'And one morning after I had—alone for once, meaning without the aid of a second sister—come to the end of a fairly uneventful night shift and there was still quite a long time until everyone was woken up, washed and had their temperatures taken, I hit on the fantastic idea of giving our old ladies' dentures a clean, but this time a thorough clean, not just with those effervescent Polident tablets. No sooner thought than done. I grabbed a metal dish and went from one bed to the next, nicking the dentures from the glasses on top of the bedside cabinets.

'When I'd collected all the false teeth I went back to the office, filled the dishes with warm water, added some detergent, took a new scrubbing brush and began, set by set, to scour my spoils. I was really giving it my all when I felt an unexpected, icy touch on my shoulder that nearly made me jump out of my skin. It was the hand of the mistress of novices, Sister Maria Augusta, who always arrived early for the first shift of the day. I hadn't reckoned with her, though. I was startled, and the metal dish slipped off my lap and clattered to the floor. Now here I was, staring at that floor, strewn with dentures, the soapy water soaking the hems of Sister Maria Augusta's and my robes, my face burning with shame because the otherwise restrained and kind-hearted Maria Augusta had just asked me, in a voice almost white with anger, whether I'd gone mad.

'At that very moment Sister Maria Imelda and Sister Maria Lucretia, who were also on the early shift, breezed into the room right on cue, and they also put their hands on their hips and stared at me accusingly. And what was I doing? I was on the verge of tears and unaware of my guilt—as yet.

'But all too soon I became aware of my crime and that I'd never again dare to look my fellow nuns in the eye, not even if my eyes suddenly straightened to punish me. For days, no weeks afterwards, we tried to attribute the dentures, which were customized and personal to each of the women, some of whom were already on the cusp of death and were spending their final years, and often only a few months, at Saint Valentine's in our, and thus my, custody. Again and again, we asked them, one after the other, to open their mouths and let us check if one set of the nearly 100 upper and lower dentures might have been hers before the demon cleaner took possession of me. Our efforts were completely in vain.

'One day, out of sheer desperation, I suggested finding the dentists who'd treated our sisters somewhere and some time. Oh, if only they had mocked, scorned and scolded me for this ludicrous suggestion! But no—lowered gazes, silence.

'Of course, I got into hot water with the Mother Superior, the hospice administration and the heads of the order too, although the latter nevertheless made sure that the more spritely older nuns were provided with new false teeth at the congregation's expense.

'Until these were ready, however, they had gruel, white bread without crusts, and tea or milky coffee for breakfast, and mashed-up food for lunch and dinner. The poor old ladies were naturally quite upset. Some of them even got depressed. Apart from the prayers we sent heavenwards for the salvation of their souls, food, the best possible food, had been the only thing that still afforded them any pleasure.

'What more can I say? Two or three weeks passed, and the New Year began. My sisters did not chastise me; they merely avoided me. They ignored my shame, even though they must have sensed how much I regretted my stupidity. I felt even lonelier than before and could barely bring myself to pray, not even alone in my cell; I never really prayed very fervently anyway, as I considered it a waste of time.

'The day came when I revealed to the Mother Superior that I did not want to complete my novitiate, choose three names and ask to profess, but would rather return to civilian life. She didn't put any obstacles in my path, even though I'd secretly but fiercely hoped she would, as I could have interpreted it as a form of forgiveness. My mistress of novices and the other sisters said goodbye to me coolly and without any fuss, not even wishing me a safe journey.

'So? What do you think now? Why did I end up here with you? Because I trained as a nurse like you did. I'm hard-working and reliable, and since that business with the dentures I've kept a lid on the overconfidence that was both my strength and my weakness. Of course I could've found a job in an ordinary German clinic, but I earn more here. That's a consolation, not my motive. When I was still a novice, the same rule that applied to all nuns applied to me—*ora et labora*; and it makes no difference whether nuns have a profession or merely profess and prostrate themselves on their knees—or sprawl full-length—from dawn till dusk before their darling Lord Jesus Christ.

'I have a standing order with my bank in Heidelberg: every month they transfer almost my entire wages to my old religious order. I want them to see that I'm doing my bit to reduce the damage I caused. It won't repair the damage, of course, especially as I don't know how much the new dentures cost and whether all of the old but still fairly vigorous sisters were taken care of, but at least it assuages my pangs of conscience.

'That ought to satisfy your curiosity, and I'd like to thank you for hearing my confession,' Stella concluded with that same smile on her face that might not actually have been one, and then drained two cups of mulled wine in quick succession. Strangely, her squint became less strong once the drink hit her bloodstream.

Stella had told us her past, thereby ensuring that she wouldn't be able to escape it, and quite possibly thought she'd made a mistake, her second mistake and every bit as impossible to rectify, since she didn't turn up for duty three days later. When we checked, her suitcase was still standing under the window, various items of clothing were tidily folded away in the wardrobe and, as her roommate Nurse Evelyn confirmed, she'd put clean sheets on her bed just the previous evening—and then left it untouched, with a well-worn teddy bear sitting on top.

Stella vanished the same way she'd appeared: unexpectedly, naturally, mysteriously. Maybe she'd tried to spin the wheel of fate and, since she was no longer a sister in a convent, didn't want to be one on a ward either. Or else some young Khalka Mongol, Buryat, Tuvan or other had glimpsed Stella, fallen hopelessly in love with her and carried her off to his province at the foot of the Altai or Tannu-Ola mountains where no one would ever find her, particularly since the Arats are not sedentary but follow their flocks of sheep, goats and yaks, as, even more acutely than the Mongolians, they can hear the whisper of the grass growing to feed them all—the livestock, and therefore the people, of this bleak and gigantic land.

None of us suspected that Sister Stella might have fallen victim to a violent crime, and if we did, we kept this thought to ourselves. 'Anyone else,' we kept reassuring one another, 'but not our squinting saint.'

Asta feels terrible; there's a strange pressure in her upper abdomen. It can't be from wandering around outside for hours. The day is gradually drawing to a close, and the sun is no longer blazing down as it did before the thunderstorm that broke as they were landing. She hasn't eaten anything dodgy either. Her last meal was breakfast in the second plane, a sticky mini-muffin. She puts out the cigarette she has only just lit and slips the 'Hugo'— her name for a stub that can still be smoked—into the side pocket of her pigskin shoulder bag.

Putting all sociophobia and logophobia aside, she thinks, if I don't want to keel over, I should take half a spin in the revolving door, look for a ladies' toilet inside, put my mouth under a tap . . .

She heads for the revolving door but then pauses after all at the steel ashtray and instead of digging out the Hugo, opens the second soft pack of her carton of duty-free cigarettes, puts a fresh Camel in her mouth and lights it. Just this one, she thinks, and then . . . I'm bound to feel better after a drink and a bite to eat. That bloody suitcase, which only contains a few faded, worn-out T-shirts anyway, can wash up in San Salvador or Madrid, for all I care. I'm going to go down to the platform, buy a ticket and take the next train to Berlin. Or first to Leipzig? I'm still officially registered there, aren't I? I'll check into a cheap hotel, apply for my pension and try to borrow money from someone. There may still be some of my final wages in my Deutsche Bank account. And don't I have an overdraft facility too?

I should really take care of all that. —What about speaking? I don't have to speak. I'll wrap a thick woollen scarf around my neck and pretend I've lost my voice. Oh sorry, voice, I know you're in there, but no one but me could and can hear you, not even the Mongolian sheep that supposedly hear the grass growing. —And if all else fails, I'll write notes.

As soon as I've got enough cash together, I'll get out of here again, and why not go back to Nicaragua? Did those arseholes at HAN officially fire me? Not that I know of. Mind you, if I did want to file an application to carry on working, they wouldn't even read it, let alone grant it. But they have no influence over where and how dear old Asta Arnold plans to spend her retirement. —I'm free, as free as a bird without wings, a metal bird, but one for which there's no longer a key, so no one can wind it up and send it skidding across the floorboards. As free as one of the moths I longed to be as a girl, even though I could see the webs under the street lamps and the spiders lurking quietly at their centre.

Yes, I'm going to stand on my own two feet. Stand on my own two feet? Isn't that, in a sense, what I've been doing my whole life? Yes, but only in a sense. Well, all right then, I'll become independent, professionally as well this time—or maybe just because I want to. What more do I need? A little rice or bean paste, a fish or a chicken from time to time, a roof of palm fronds over my head, a few utensils to impress people, a range of drops, ointments and pills in pretty bottles, tins and boxes with German labels. I'll open a kind of first-aid post near San Juan del Sur, on Playa El Coco or Playa La Flor where I administer to the Nicas for a handful of centavos or payment in kind, pulling out splinters, treating wounds, soothing scorpion bites, tackling infections, bringing down fevers—and applying casts to simple fractures; it's not as if I've no experience of doing those things.

And once I feel confident and daring enough to do more and take on minor operations, who's going to stop me?! I'll play the wise white woman, the mystical, mute healer. I may be a little crazy, but I'm smart and the only reason I didn't become a doctor was because it was too much responsibility. —Oh right, I didn't have a high-school diploma either.

Who cares, I've nothing to fear, nothing to lose, only a decent chance—just like the Nicas, because they can get an X-ray and a diagnosis free in one of the UNESCO-funded clinics, but they still have to break their piggybanks for medicine and lengthy treatment. And it's a long way to the larger towns, to the places where those clinics are located, too far, especially between the months of May and December when the pickups and battered old buses can barely make it along dirt roads the never-ending rains have turned to mud or even flooded.

I'll build up such a good reputation that the young US and European backpackers and surfers who've started to crowd Nicaragua's beaches during the dry season will want to make use of my services too. They rarely have travel insurance but they do often have the odd graze, bruise, upset tummy, earache, circulatory dis-order, lovesickness; simple ailments in any case—and not much money, though more than the Nicas.

That's it, that's the way it'll be: foreigners will pay in cash, locals with meat, vegetables, fish and eggs; the only thing I'll turn down are turtle eggs. My Nicas will finally have to realize that they're taboo.

Maybe Manfred will help me to look for an apartment or an afford-able plot of land for my hut; apparently he has excellent contacts all over Latin America.

Manfred, the old Lothario and aid worker; a few years ago he could have been one of those people on the other side of the glass wall. Since he retired, though, he's given up his globetrotting and spends most of his time on his coffee plantation near San Juan del Norte. —When did I last see him? If I remember rightly, it was ten months ago at a birthday party for his younger brother, Doctor Wilhelm Maiwald, a surgeon who worked for us at HAN for a few weeks.

What might old Manfred be up to right now, as I stand here, fighting back a peculiar urge to vomit, not even fancying a cigarette? I see him lying in his hammock next to his wooden villa; he's gazing down at the Pacific, sucking on a Casa de Torres, with his current Nica-Lolita tousling his greying chest fleece. —Why such poisonous thoughts? Because when I met him in a tapas bar on 8 August 2011 and he invited me that same evening to come and visit him soon please, I assumed that he liked or perhaps even desired me. He was 72 at the time, and I was a mere 61. Had I really imagined that that was young enough for a man like him in a land like that?

He wanted, he said when I did visit him, to practise his German. And that's what he did, all week long. He prattled away without any pause for breath about his heroic deeds, his fabulous life, his more or less imaginary gout. He loved having his pulse taken every few seconds. 'Your fingers,' he moaned, 'are so wonderfully cool.' And one night, when I'd nodded off during one of his monologues, he squawked into my ear that he had one heartfelt desire—'Königsberg meatballs.'

OK, so I cooked some for him, also pea soup, roulade, goulash and a Rhineland pot roast that I'd marinated myself, of course; after all, I was his guest and, I thought, still a woman.

For the pot roast of all things Manfred invited a man he'd met that lunchtime in his favourite *cantina* while I was at the *mercado* searching for decent cut of beef, and now called his 'only true friend here', a former East German merchant navy sailor.

Peter—tall, broad, with a purple potato nose—turned up about two hours late, around ten in the evening, with his girlfriend Fernanda, a thin and sad-looking Nicaraguan who, he stressed, had been born in Los Credees, only three villages away from Manfred's estate. He'd fallen for her beauty on one of his final voyages before East Germany collapsed. She'd been some kind of kitchen help on his ship, the MS *Meissen*, 'a maid of all work, actually,' he added cheerfully and pulled Fernanda towards him, eliciting a shrill cry from her because she was wearing her right arm in a pillow case folded into a triangle and tied behind her long black hair.

'The arm's broken,' Peter said almost proudly, 'but it's a clean fracture, no complications at all. The guy who took the X-rays reckoned it will practically heal by itself. All we had to do was immobilize the arm slightly.' His Fernanda, he explained, was unfortunately a little clumsy and had fallen down the stairs three days ago while cleaning.

'What stairs?' Manfred asked, grinning. 'You live in a bungalow that's as flat as a flounder.'

'Oh, it didn't happen at home!' Peter cried in outrage. 'Women and men are equal in my house. Which is why my princess has to bring home a little extra. I send her out twice a week to clean for a law firm in Rivas, a three-storey building that's sumptuous for these parts. I know the boss pretty well, a Frenchman. He gave me that half-rotten, not fully paid-off motorboat I use from time to time to take tourists out to Ometepe Island and potter around looking for marlins to catch.'

Manfred waggled his head dubiously. I too thought, Uhuh, that can't be true. Maybe Peter here was drunk and maltreated his girl-friend.

'Where are the X-rays?' I asked. I still spoke sometimes then.

'In our kitchen, next to the bread tin!' cried Peter, clearly happy that he could remember.

Furrowing my brow, I laid 300 córdobas on Peter's clean-licked plate. 'Tomorrow you're going to go to the pharmacy, buy Vaseline, 25 bandages for a cast, a double sling with a Velcro fastening, another cushioned one if they have them, and a packet of paracetamol,' I said. 'And please don't forget the X-rays! Once you've got all of that together, come back here and I'll do the rest.'

And they did actually return the next evening with everything I'd ordered. Peter even seemed sober. I sent him and Manfred out of the house. I'd be better off without their company for what needed doing next.

Manfred came back, though. He ambled towards the bathroom past Fernanda and me and tried to grab the 11-year-old Ron de Nicaragua I'd bought for my patient and hidden under the dirty washing. But the expression of fake innocence on his face betrayed him. I pushed him away. It turned out that he had a secret stash too: in the cupboard by the corner sofa were five bottles of single malt! He took out two of them, shot me an extra-smug look, locked the cupboard, removed the key and finally disappeared, at least for the time being.

I set down a large glass of Ron de Nicaragua in front of Fernanda; she emptied it and, her features still twisted with pain, took off her light dress, which luckily had a wide neck and would therefore be easy to pull on over the plaster cast. I examined the X-rays, which did indeed show a nice, clean fracture of the humerus, Fernanda's strangely twisted shoulders and her bruised and swollen upper arm.

'Ready?' I asked. She gave me an anxious nod, so I immediately pushed five paracetamol between her teeth and, for good measure, the holed end of the leather belt. I signalled to her to bite hard on it while I rubbed the vaseline into the downy skin of her broken arm, since otherwise, when the plaster hardened later on, it would give the hairs a nasty tweak, then I bent her arm and placed three thick books as supports. Once this was done, I fetched the soaked bandages from the bathroom and got winding as I had learnt to do, not very tight and moving downwards from shoulder to wrist.

Fernanda looked relieved even before my work had dried enough for me to put it in the double sling, and she treated herself to a generous swig of rum straight from the bottle. Only then did she fill the glass still standing next to the books on the table to the brim and passed it to me, very dexterously, I thought, especially as, unlike me, she wasn't left-handed.

It was a long night; Fernanda sang revolutionary songs, Peter told stories, not particularly fluently, of life in the East German merchant navy and how pissed off they'd always been because they were never allowed to go ashore in a 'capitalist port', and Manfred cracked jokes.

When Fernanda and Peter had left, Manfred looked at me differently, sort of normally and maybe a little admiringly, perhaps even with pride.

Fernanda's broken bone must have long since healed, and her right arm must be as strong as before. I don't know for sure, though, because my leave came to an end soon after I'd treated her; I had to return to the capital.

I had advised Fernanda to keep the plaster on for at least one month and then to have it carefully removed with the aid of a machete, poultry shears or something of that ilk. —For my first-aid post I'll definitely need some kind of small electric circular saw; I should be able to get one in a specialist shop or from an old orthopaedist looking to close his surgery. —If only I didn't feel so nauseous. I can hardly think straight any more.

Soon though, very soon indeed, I'll have a nice life. Early in the morning I'll crawl out of my soft bed, brew myself some coffee, Turkish, no milk. Cup in hand, I'll walk barefoot to the beach. Grey pelicans will be circling in the sky; but now, against the rising sun, they look like black cut-outs. One spots some prey and drops out of the air, as fast and heavy as a stone. For a few seconds I see the glittering silver fish, then only something wriggling in the pelican's baggy beak pouch as it takes off again with leisurely, expansive wing beats and disappears to some place where it can digest in peace or feed its young and where my eyes cannot follow it.

I sit down, smoke a cigarette, gaze at the wet sand, bubbling suspiciously in places, and smoke the next and wait—until a few crabs venture out of their holes, their eyes popping out on stems at me, and they wave their pincers as a threat or in greeting and eventually sidle off to hide away again, this time under one of the three or four bone-white mangrove trunks that have been knocked over by a storm and licked clean by seawater.

A dog would be good—and easy to find. I walk along the nearest village street or skirt the ocean and come across whole packs of stray mutts, mongrels of all sizes, all colours, all ages. But there are also these not yet completely feral loners, their fundamental trust in our species inexplicably intact. You only have to look into one of these dogs' eyes and it will follow you as if you were its mother. I'll find it, my dog, a young one with short, light-coloured fur, a dark muzzle, an innocent face and funny floppy ears.

Oh God, I'm about to puke. But not here, not by the revolving door . . .

T he time has come. Asta can't wait a second longer; she has to go, whether she likes it or not. Her nausea is so intense that she rushes into the doorway and beats on the wing glass in front of her to make it spin more quickly. Nothing's working now, because for what seems like an unbearably long time to Asta, these panicked blows bring about exactly the opposite of what she meant to achieve—until she realizes why she is trapped and lowers her arms and takes a step back. This breaks the blockage, and Asta rushes across the lounge, pushing aside anyone in her path, towards the familiar glowing emerald-green pictogram that oddly, right now, reminds her of a piece from a board game. It looks like a Ludo-man or rather a Ludo-woman, she thinks.

Asta has reached her goal and doesn't need to queue—a cubicle is free. She goes in, locks it and bends over the toilet bowl, but nothing comes out. Someone flushes in the cubicle to Asta's right. Or is it automatic, she wonders. She's having trouble breathing, but nevertheless tries to hold in the air. Her knees buckle, she crumples and collapses to the floor. Little dots dance before her eyes. No, glow-worms, she thinks; haven't seen any of those for years. Something's constricting my chest, must be my bra. It's from the flea market by Santiago de Managua cathedral and it's too tight. Wasn't really one anywhere there that fit. How wildly my heart is pounding—and so weirdly irregularly. Could be a myocardial infarction. Front wall? Back wall? —I might be close to kicking the bucket, and I can think of no better words than 'none' and 'no'. —'Kick the bucket' is a slang term, so is 'pushing up the daisies'. There are no buckets here, no daisies either. Never liked those flowers. —Oops, my bra's just torn. Or else the invisible giant fist that's slowly squeezing the life out of me has eased off. Still, can't take a deep breath; the fist's closing again, not quickly but steadily.

It's a heart attack for sure, thinks Asta, acute coronary syndrome. —Did I lock the toilet door? Yes. Nobody can get in, not any time soon. They'd just stare stupidly rather than fetching a defibrillator. —Find a different ear, voice. Take care, Rosita, my little, my only, my true sister whom I haven't seen for ages, who didn't want to see me. —Well, well, I think of you and the fist pauses. Is it scared perhaps? Of you? Or of me? Weren't you scared when our father, *the temper tornado*, as Granny called him, didn't hit me for the first time but you, because you'd taken the blame for one of my wrongdoings? I kept quiet, didn't defend you, and so betrayed you. I cut loose, also for the first time, yet I've been doing it almost every day since and now I'm cutting loose for good.

Asta pushes her shoulder bag under her head and her right hand between her breasts; with the left she clasps the duty-free bag. There are still nine packets of Camels in there, she thinks, eight full and one open, one hundred and seventy-nine cigarettes. Pity I won't be able to smoke them now . . .

—THE END—